The Amazing Wilmer Dooley

Also by Fowler DeWitt

The Contagious Colors of Mumpley Middle School

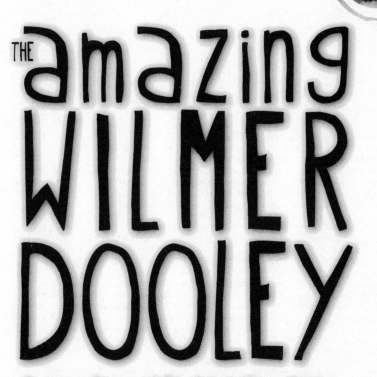

THE amazing WILMER DOOLEY

a mumpley middle school mystery

by FOWLER DeWiTT   illustrated by RODOLFO MONTALVO

𝒜
atheneum

ATHENEUM BOOKS FOR YOUNG READERS · New York London Toronto Sydney New Delhi

𝒜
atheneum

ATHENEUM BOOKS FOR YOUNG READERS
An imprint of Simon & Schuster Children's Publishing Division
1230 Avenue of the Americas, New York, New York 10020

ATHENEUM BOOKS FOR YOUNG READERS is a registered trademark of ʹSimon & Schuster, Inc.
Atheneum logo is a trademark of Simon & Schuster, Inc.
For information about special discounts for bulk purchases, please contact Simon & Schuster Special Sales at 1-866-506-1949 or business@simonandschuster.com.
The Simon & Schuster Speakers Bureau can bring authors to your live event. For more information or to book an event, contact the Simon & Schuster Speakers Bureau at 1-866-248-3049 or visit our website at www.simonspeakers.com.
Book design by Lauren Rille
The text for this book is set in Excelsior.
The illustrations for this book are rendered in pen and ink, brush, and digital color.
Manufactured in the United States of America
0714 FFG
First Edition
10 9 8 7 6 5 4 3 2 1
Library of Congress Cataloging-in-Publication Data
DeWitt, Fowler.
The amazing Wilmer Dooley : a Mumpley Middle School mystery / by Fowler DeWitt ; illustrated by Rodolfo Montalvo. — 1st ed.
p. cm.
Summary: Hoping to impress Roxie with his dazzling project on bacteria, seventh-grader-to-be Wilmer Dooley enters the state science fair, where he encounters his archnemesis, Claudius, who may be planning something terribly sinister.
ISBN 978-1-4424-9854-9 (hardcover)
ISBN 978-1-4424-9856-3 (eBook)
[1. Science—Methodology—Fiction. 2. Science fairs—Fiction. 3. Mystery and detective stories.] I. Montalvo, Rodolfo, illustrator. II. Title.
PZ7.D526Am 2014
[Fic]—dc23 2013033177

To my long-lost Samantha.
I should have listened. The alligators *were* hungry.
–F. D.

To my brothers, Eulizes and Jonathan
–R. M.

The Amazing Wilmer Dooley

CHAPTER ONE

Dear Wilmer,
    You're almost a seventh grader
now! The new school year starts
in only two weeks. Oh, son—you're
growing up so fast! Did you know
a blue whale baby gains almost
two hundred pounds a day? You're
not growing THAT fast, thankfully.
We wouldn't have enough fish
in the house to feed you. Your
mother and I know you'll have
a great time at the science fair
this weekend. Remember, winning
isn't everything. What's important
is that you learn lots of science.
So relax. Have fun. And, most of
all, observe!
    Love,
    Dad

Wilmer jammed an extra pair of underwear into his
canvas overnight bag, and a spare pair of science
goggles. Scientists should never be without enough

underwear or goggles, even for a short weekend trip. "Do you think four pairs of underwear is enough?" Wilmer asked.

His best friend, Ernie, sat on Wilmer's bed. Ernie's black hair stood straight up, but the rest of him seemed slightly sleepy. He yawned. "We're going to be away for two days. Are you expecting some sort of underwear emergency?"

Wilmer shot Ernie a dirty look. Still, he packed a fifth pair, just in case. A scientist needed to be ready for anything.

Wilmer wanted to haul even more scientific equipment along for the weekend. But his precious beakers and vials could break, and his magnifying glass didn't magnify very much. The best scientists in the state would be attending the science fair. Wilmer didn't want to carry around second-class equipment.

Besides, he had to lug all the materials for his exhibit in a large box, which was already bulky and heavy.

"The Forty-Fifth Annual State Science Fair and Consortium!" Wilmer shot Ernie a big grin. "Aren't you excited?"

Ernie didn't answer.

"I said, aren't you excited?" Wilmer repeated louder.

Ernie cradled an iNoise, his thumbs flicking. He looked up, annoyed. "Ah, c'mon! You made me mess up my game."

"Don't you get sick of that thing? You're on it all the time."

"Do you get sick of your nose? It's on your face all the time."

"Of course not."

"Exactly. And my iNoise is way cooler than your nose, believe me." Ernie grinned and turned his attention once again to his small handheld device.

The iNoise played games and music, took pictures and video, had a built-in GPS and voice-activated instant messaging, and, if you put it on bread, made toast. It was the hottest must-have electronic gadget of the summer.

But Wilmer didn't need or want an iNoise—he had the power of observation! That was all any scientist really needed.

Still, Wilmer may have been the only incoming seventh grader in his entire school without one.

Wilmer zipped his bag and folded the top of his cardboard box shut. He was bringing a slide-show projector, elaborate retractable fiberglass stands with detailed bacteria facts printed on them, a ten-minute video on the history of germs, six jars of glowing foods and one filled with leeches, and a bunch of other disease-based show-and-tells.

Wilmer was especially proud of the leeches—slimy worms used by medieval doctors. They had been difficult to find. Wilmer would put them on his arm and demonstrate how they sucked out blood.

Or maybe not. Thinking of those oozing creatures on his skin made Wilmer squeamish. But he would do just about anything to win first place, even if it meant tolerating slimy blood-slurping.

"I can't believe you put so much work into your exhibit," said Ernie, shaking his head.

"You can't win first place unless you try your hardest. What's your project?"

"I hooked a potato up with some wires. The

energy from the potato turns on a lightbulb." Ernie held up a shoe box. "I found directions online."

"That's not going to win first place."

"Yeah, but it only took me an hour," said Ernie, "which meant more time to play games on my iNoise."

Wilmer sighed. He knew that the other competitors wouldn't take the contest so lightly. The Annual State Science Fair and Consortium was legendary. You had to be the best of the best to participate. It was by invitation only: a teacher needed to officially nominate you.

Biology teacher Mrs. Padgett had nominated Wilmer. That had been a surprise. Valveeta Padgett, the chair of the school Science Department (co-chair of the school Detention Program, and co-co-chair of the school Chair Cleaning Committee) didn't seem to like him very much.

The feeling was mutual.

But maybe she had changed for the better. After all, Mrs. Padgett wasn't just a teacher anymore—she was now a star, appearing in her own weekend television morning show, *Padgett!*, which mixed biology and online mah-jongg.

It was an odd combination, but somehow, it worked.

"The science fair is in a brand-new location this year," said Wilmer. He held his official nomination letter. "Don't you think the place sounds fancy? Ernie? Ernie?"

Ernie looked up from his iNoise. "Oh, come on! You made me lose again!"

"Your brain's going to turn to mush if you play that too much," warned Wilmer.

"Cool," said Ernie. "I like mush." He kept playing.

"I heard Roxie is go-glighh," said Wilmer. He meant to say "going," but the last word caught in his throat and came out as a gurgle. Just thinking of Roxie turned *his* brain into mush. Roxie had long flowing blond hair, twinkling blue eyes (Wilmer preferred to think of them as low-melanin-pigmented eyes), and white teeth that sparkled like a Bunsen burner. He hadn't seen her since school ended.

"Did you call Roxie this summer?" asked Ernie.

"No. I was too busy with my science project."

"Too wimpy, you mean."

Wilmer didn't argue.

"Claudius is going to the fair too," said Wilmer, trying to clear his mind of Roxie. It did the trick: if Roxie made Wilmer think of tulips and rosebuds, Claudius stirred up images of dark, stormy clouds and fungus.

Wilmer and Claudius had worked together to cure the awful contagious colors that had swept through Mumpley Middle School last year. But that didn't make them friends—far from it.

"I heard two other Mumpley kids are going," said Ernie, putting his iNoise in his pocket. "A sixth grader and a new transfer student."

"I just hope we learn lots of science," said Wilmer. His father always told him that learning was more important than winning.

"That sounds horrible," groaned Ernie. "I just want to jump on the beds, stay up late eating snacks, and play with my iNoise."

Wilmer rolled his eyes. "This is a weekend for science, not goofing off."

"For you, maybe," said Ernie. "I'm all about the goofing. I don't even know why Mrs. Padgett nominated me," he added with a frown.

Wilmer gave his best friend a harmless shoulder punch. "You were nominated because you deserve to go. You helped solve the Mumpley malady last year. I couldn't have done it without you."

"I guess," said Ernie. "But—"

"No 'buts,'" interrupted Wilmer. "We'll hang out together all weekend. I'll make sure you have a good time."

Ernie threw Wilmer a thankful grin and the two exchanged their secret best friend thumbshake: two pumps followed by a thumbs-up.

"Are you two ready?" called Mrs. Dooley from downstairs. "Your father is waiting!"

"Coming!" yelled Wilmer. He grabbed his overnight bag and inched his unwieldy box toward the door. "Can you give me a hand?" he asked Ernie.

Ernie smiled. "Electronic potatoes," he said, tossing his shoe box lightly in the air and catching it. "Who's laughing now?"

Wilmer nudged his box a few centimeters farther. A weekend of science! It would be magnificent.

So why couldn't he remove the sneaking suspicion that something was going to go horribly wrong? And that that something wrong had a name: Claudius Dill.

CHAPTER TWO

Science Consortium Packing Checklist
   By Wilmer Dooley

      Projector
      Fiberglass stands
      Video player
      Jars of glowing foods
      14 hungry leeches (in a jar)
      Science goggles
      ~~Magnifying Glass~~
      ~~Four~~ Five pairs of underwear
      The power of observation!
      My lucky Albert Einstein socks
      Funny science jokes (to impress Roxie)

Mr. Dooley stood next to the family station wagon.
He wore a lab coat and no pants or shoes. Wilmer

was used to his dad's absentmindedness, but forgetting to put on pants was a little extreme, even for him.

Mr. Ignatius P. Dooley was a world-renowned scientist, celebrated for the invention of Sugar-BUZZZZ!, the wondrous line of snacks and drinks that came in twelve fluorescently colored flavors. More recently he had created VeggiBUZZZZ! This new line of glowing vegetables made healthy eating fun, even sort of cool, and had become an immediate sensation.

Wilmer still preferred his plain everyday green spinach to the vibrantly glowing pink variety his dad had created. But most kids strongly disagreed.

"Nice legs, Dad," Wilmer said.

Wilmer's father looked down at his bare, hairy limbs. "I had a small polyester fire in the lab. I'm afraid my trousers took the worst of it." He held up a small swatch of glowing violet fabric. "Clothes-BUZZZZ!" he announced. His voice switched to a low radio baritone: "Why wear regular old clothes when yours can glow like a thousand streetlamps? Night jogging has never been safer. Imagine how easy it will be to find your kids at the mall. Make a statement with ClothesBUZZZZ! And that statement is: 'Look at me! I glow in the dark!'"

Wilmer shrugged. "Sounds like a winner, Dad."

Mr. Dooley nodded his head. "If only the clothes didn't spontaneously burst into flames. Or cause horrible boils to erupt all over your skin." He rolled up the right sleeve of his lab coat to reveal a dozen red bumps covering his arm. "Do you think that's a problem?"

Wilmer nodded. "I think that's a deal-killer, Dad."

Mr. Dooley frowned. "That's what I feared. Well, a scientist's work is never done. Are you two ready to go to the science fair?"

"We sure are," said Wilmer with an excited grin as Ernie yawned. "But I still think you need to wear pants and shoes."

Mr. Dooley sighed and jogged back to the house while Wilmer and Ernie loaded the car with their luggage. Wilmer's father trotted past Mrs. Dooley, who was walking briskly down the driveway with their younger sons in tow. Wilmer's short, thin, and rosy-cheeked mother carried a plastic food container. She loved to cook and bake, and her concoctions were always original, sometimes brilliant, but usually dreadful.

"I can't believe you're leaving us for a whole weekend!" she wept. She handed her container to Ernie and wrapped Wilmer in a bear hug. "My little Wilmer-Poo is all grown up!"

Wilmer squirmed out of his mother's grasp, his face turning as red as one of his father's Veggi-BUZZZZ! tomatoes.

Mrs. Dooley turned to Wilmer's brothers and wagged her finger at them sternly. "Don't just stand there," she ordered. "Hug your brother good-bye."

"Do we have to?" complained seven-year-old Sherman. Mrs. Dooley's frown answered his question. Sherman put an unenthusiastic arm around Wilmer, who awkwardly hugged him back.

"What's in here, Mrs. Dooley?" asked Ernie, sniffing the food container she had handed him. "It smells like oranges, vinegar, and horseradish."

"That's because they're orange, vinegar, and

horseradish brownies," said Mrs. Dooley proudly. "With a smidgen of yarn."

"Onion salt!" yelped her youngest son, twenty-month-old Preston.

"Yes, and a dash of onion salt," confirmed Mrs. Dooley. "And really, that makes all the difference." Preston smiled proudly. He often assisted Mrs. Dooley in her cooking.

Wilmer turned slightly green, but Ernie licked his lips. "They sound delicious, Mrs. D." Ernie loved sweets even more than Wilmer loved creamed spinach.

Preston wrapped both his arms around Wilmer in a heartfelt good-bye hug. "Garlic powder!" he shouted with sincerity.

"Um, you too," said Wilmer.

The front door of the house banged open and Mr. Dooley bounded toward them. He now wore a bright green-and-blue pair of mermaid-patterned shorts and winter boots. Wilmer didn't think they were much of an improvement over his earlier wardrobe choices, but at least his dad wouldn't be arrested.

Mrs. Dooley blew her nose and wiped her tears while Wilmer, Ernie, and Mr. Dooley piled into the station wagon. Soon the three were waving good-bye and heading down the driveway.

"You know," said Mr. Dooley as they pulled onto the main road, "I entered this same science fair when I was your age." He scratched his forehead. "No, I'm thinking of the summer I visited your Aunt Ethel's cattle farm."

"Aunt Ethel is a truck driver," said Wilmer.

"Well, something like that." Mr. Dooley then proceeded to tell a long, boring story about his failed attempts at creating fluorescent livestock.

Ernie popped open the plastic top from Mrs. Dooley's container. It sat on the seat between them. He lifted a brownie and deeply inhaled its overbearing horseradish scent. "Want one?" he asked Wilmer.

Wilmer's stomach voiced a loud objection, and he grimaced with disgust. Ernie shrugged and chomped down on the gloppy treat.

"How is it?" asked Wilmer.

Ernie swallowed. "A bit too much yarn." He picked some string out of his teeth.

Wilmer looked out the window. They still had a couple more hours of driving. He was sure this would be the best weekend of his life, if only that nagging suspicion of trouble would dissolve, like sulfur in a jar of carbon disulfide.

CHAPTER THREE

Dear Journal,

    I know I haven't written in a while. I've been try-
ing to learn all about diseases, now that I've decided
to become a doctor someday instead of a scientist. I
almost feel guilty going to this conference for future
scientists! But doctors and scientists have lots in
common. They both wear white lab coats. One says
"Aha!" when making discoveries, and the other says
"Ahhhh!" when holding a tongue depressor.

    Scientific journals and medical journals are really
similar too. Which means that keeping a scientific
journal is pretty much the same thing as keeping a
medical journal. So no more excuses for not writing.

    We're driving up to the science consortium right
now. Ernie is playing on his iNoise. What a waste of time!
Why play games when you can do things like memo-
rize the scientific names for birds?

European robin: *Erithacus rubecula*
American crow: *Corvus brachyrhynchos*
See? Isn't that fun?

I'm a bit nervous about seeing Roxie. She's not entering the science contest. She'll be reporting for the school newspaper and for *Monday Mumpley Musings*, her biweekly school-broadcast radio show.

I should have seen her this summer like I promised. I'm just a big chicken. People should call me Jersey Giant, which is the largest breed of chicken, weighing eleven to thirteen pounds.

Scientific name: *Gallus gallus domesticus*

It'll be nice to get away from town. Sure, I helped find a cure for that disease. But were the appearance on the evening news, the newspaper articles, and the honorary Wilmer Dooley Day parade really necessary? The papers are calling me 'The Amazing Wilmer Dooley'! People keep asking to shake my hand. It's nice, unless they've been picking their nose or eating fried chicken, which is why I usually carry hand sanitizer. It's weird getting so much attention. I guess this is how celebrities feel.

But I'm not a celebrity. I'm just an observant scientist. And someone who likes clean hands.
Signing off,
Wilmer Dooley

Wilmer, Ernie, and Mr. Dooley stood inside the main lobby of the Sac à Puces Palladium, Lodge, and Resortlike Hotel. The French name was the nicest thing about the place. It smelled like mold. The walls and low ceiling were cracking, the wallpaper was peeling, and the lights were dim and dreary. The brown carpeting was worn and frayed. The framed paintings on the wall were all of sailboats, which was nice until you looked closely and realized the sailboats were sinking, many with sharks close by.

"Man, this place is a pit," said Ernie. "I thought you said this was a fancy hotel."

"No, I said this placed *sounded* fancy," said Wilmer with a forced smile. Still, his disappointment ran deep.

The lobby teemed with the finest kid scientists in the state: the smartest of the smart, the geekiest of the geeks. Some seemed serious, wearing thick glasses and holding personal science journals or electronic tablets for note-taking. Other kids, however, ran around, yelling and pushing and bumping into people. Wilmer frowned. Future scientists shouldn't just run amok.

A good scientist was in control of his emotions at all times.

Mr. Dooley rested his hand on Wilmer's shoulder and gave his son a soft, encouraging squeeze. "Are you sure you have everything? Didn't forget your toothbrush or hairbrush, your goggles or your pocket protector?"

"I'm good," said Wilmer.

"Most importantly, don't forget to observe!"

"I won't. Don't worry, Dad. I'll make you proud."

"You always do," said Mr. Dooley. He sniffled and wiped a tear from his eye. "Oh, I envy you two!" he exclaimed. "Just you and science, floating in the seas of perception, drowning in the tides of discovery, swimming in the squall of invention, and rolling in the rocking waters of wit! And, if you'll excuse me, I have to go to the bathroom."

Mr. Dooley hurried off, narrowly avoiding three sprinting kids as he weaved his way across the crowded lobby.

Ernie pointed. "Over there. Three o'clock. Claudius Dill."

Claudius stood across the room. Wilmer stared darts at his nemesis. He wished he could throw darts at him, too—but his eyes would need to suffice. Claudius chatted with a kid who shared Claudius's straight dark hair, swampy green eyes, and despicable scowl. In fact, they were practically twins, except that this new kid was much heavier than Claudius and better dressed, with ironed slacks and a bow tie.

As if having one Claudius-sized Claudius wasn't bad enough, Wilmer dreaded meeting an extra-large, fancier version of him.

Next to regular Claudius and plump Claudius stood a tall, imposing-looking man. Wilmer recognized him as the famous Dr. Fernando Dill, Claudius's father and the World's Greatest Doctor, according to a recent award.

Claudius looked at Wilmer. Wilmer stared back at Claudius. Claudius sneered. Wilmer sneered too. If the heat of hate was as hot as the sun, which is approximately ten thousand degrees Fahrenheit on its surface according to most calculations, the whole room would have melted on the spot.

Claudius seethed, steam practically rising from his ears like an overheated teapot. Wilmer Dooley! The name sat in his craw like a lump of stale green gelatin. Claudius knew Wilmer was invited to the consortium weekend, but he had hoped Wilmer would have gotten lost, been sick, over-slept, or better still, been eaten by armadillos.

But no such luck!

Wilmer—that show-off—was probably here to brag:

Look at me! I cured Mumpley Middle School! I'm good and kind and help people, because kittens are fuzzy and warm blankets are snuggly.

It was enough to make a guy sick.

"The Amazing Wilmer Dooley," that's what

the papers were calling him now. Simply horrible. "Amazing" and "Wilmer" didn't belong together in the same sentence, unless that sentence was, "Everyone hates the amazingly annoying Wilmer Dooley."

And what had Wilmer done to be anointed "amazing," anyway? Save a few hundred kids from certain death? Big deal. Wilmer didn't even deserve to attend this science weekend. But Claudius did. He'd earned *his* invitation by coming to school every Friday during summer vacation and emptying Mrs. Padgett's garbage can. True, it was already empty since no one attended school over the summer. Still, he needed to make amends. He had momentarily revolted against Mrs. Padgett and joined alliances with Wilmer to save the school last year. That had been a lapse of judgment. All it did was make Wilmer a hero.

But Claudius was a hero too! It was so unfair— not even a single magazine article had been written about him.

Well, no. There had been one article: "People

Who Know Wilmer Dooley but Who Are Otherwise Unimportant." Claudius was quoted as saying, "Wilmer Dooley is my hero. I'm his biggest fan. I am! I am!" Upon reading it, Claudius had ripped the article into tiny shreds and then gagged. They had it terribly wrong! What he had *actually* said was, "Wilmer Dooley? I'm eating a hero," referring to the ham-and-cheese sub sandwich he had ordered at the deli, which had a broken air conditioner. "This place needs a bigger fan. I love ham! I love ham!" He should have known the reporter would get it wrong. That Gwendolyn Bray, the star news reporter, was barely paying attention when Claudius spoke. She was too busy primping her hair and playing with her old-fashioned tape recorder.

Claudius needed to put Wilmer in his place. He would start by winning the science fair this weekend, if only because that meant Wilmer wouldn't. First place was a brand-new, top-of-the-line 1,000X binocular compound digital microscope with a 360-degree swiveling head and multidimensional time-lapse imaging. Quite pricey, actually. Claudius had four of them at home. But he wanted to win first place to make Wilmer squirm, not for any stupid prize.

Claudius's cousin Vlad stood next to him. He was transferring to Mumpley Middle School this year. Vlad was quite the scientist, or so Dr. Dill had often said.

Vlad and Claudius had worked together on their science fair project. Claudius had wanted to power a lightbulb with a potato, but Vlad had a different idea. Claudius had to admit, his cousin's plan was better. And more diabolical.

Claudius grinned to himself. He loved to carry out sinister schemes. He even wore an EVIL GENIUS T-shirt under his sweater.

Dr. Dill put his arms around Vlad and Claudius. The science consortium needed parent chaperones, and Claudius's father had surprisingly volunteered. Dr. Dill was normally too busy to do anything involving Claudius, including paying attention to him, or remembering his birthday or his name. "Looking forward to the weekend, Clavicle?" he asked.

"That's Claudius, Dad," said Claudius.

"'Claudius Dad.' What a strange name. Are you sure? Well, you should know," muttered Dr. Dill. "Just try to be more like your cousin and I'm sure you'll do fine." He gave Vlad a hearty clap on the back.

"Thanks, Dr. Dill," said Vlad, straightening his bow tie.

The sounds of Beethoven's ninth symphony flew from the doctor's sports jacket pocket, and he quickly fished out his mobile. "Good thing I have my special phone. I get reception everywhere!" He answered the call. "Dr. Dill here . . . He has a severe case of Bottle Neck? I see. Is he congested?" He turned his back on the boys and wandered away, deep in conversation.

Vlad pointed across the floor and Claudius followed his cousin's outstretched finger. If it were a laser beam, it would have bored a hole right through Wilmer Dooley. "Isn't that Dooley?" he asked. Claudius had told his cousin of his hatred for Wilmer. "Is he waving us over?"

Wilmer had his hand up and *was* waving. Ugh. He probably thought they were friends now. Claudius shivered. Well, he might as well get this over with—they would be seeing Wilmer all weekend.

But Claudius had plans. He wouldn't only win first place; he would put Wilmer in his place, too. Claudius giggled at the thought of his devious scheme. He reached under his sweater to feel the bottom of his hidden EVIL GENIUS T-shirt.

Vlad eyed Claudius, smiled, and then echoed Claudius's cackle.

CHAPTER FOUR

A Love Poem for Roxie McGhee
   By Wilmer Dooley

   I think that I shall never see
   A girl as lovely as Roxie McGhee.
   With eyes of blue and hair of gold,
   Our love will grow like common slime mold.

Note: needs work. Is there a better word for "gold"?

Wilmer watched regular Claudius and plump Claudius amble over. Why were they approaching? Did they think he had waved them over? Wilmer had merely yawned and stretched his arm.

   "And who are you?" asked Ernie, shooting Vlad an evil eye. "Claudius's extra-large clone?"

   Vlad tugged his bow tie and returned the evil

glare, but with considerably more nastiness. Ernie gasped and shrank back. "I'm your worst nightmare. My name is Vladimir Despicopovitz. My cousin and I are going to win the science fair this weekend. And I promise you it will blow your mind." He giggled. Claudius giggled even harder.

Wilmer eyed Vlad and Claudius carefully. Those two were up to something, and that meant they were up to something bad. He would have to keep an even closer eye on them than he'd planned.

But Wilmer didn't want to keep his eyes on the two troublemakers right then. He much preferred to keep them on Roxie, who was walking up with a friendly hello.

She wore a pink sweater and pink headband. She reminded Wilmer of a fragrant pink rose, glistening on a meadow under the dazzling rays of the morning sun, and a bunch of other gooey things. Headphones hung around her neck. She also held a microphone, and had a small electronic gadget strapped to her waist. She noticed the boys staring at it.

"Do you like this? It's a tape recorder. It's

practically an antique, but it's just like the one
Gwendolyn Bray uses. She's my hero, you know."
Her voice rang like a delicate glass bell, its chime
dancing softly in Wilmer's ear canals. "We're here at
the state science fair! Can you believe it? I bet you
guys will do great. Especially you, Wilmer." Wilmer
blushed and looked down at his sneakers, before
daring to sneak a peek back up.

Roxie smiled at Wilmer. He smiled back. Well,
actually, he tried to smile back, but he wanted to
shoot her a particularly handsome and suave smile
so he tried curling his lip, but feared it looked more
like a deranged sneer than a smile. Roxie seemed
confused and glanced away. Wilmer bit his lip to
keep it from curling again.

"Where are my manners? Do you guys know
Harriet Scruggs?" said Roxie. She stepped to
the side, revealing a small, mousy girl standing
behind her.

So *this* was the sixth grader who had been
nominated from Mumpley Middle School: child
prodigy Harriet Scruggs.

Wilmer glared at her. Harriet had recently

won a major national science award. She would be Wilmer's stiffest competition this weekend.

She wore a pink sweater and pink headband that were sort of like Roxie's, except the sweater was too long and the headband was a different, uglier shade of pink. She had an impossibly large nose and giant teeth that hung over her bottom lip.

Harriet gave a small wave. "Ar-ar-are you the Amazing Wilmer Dooley?" she stuttered.

Wilmer nodded and narrowed his eyes as he faced this new threat to his first-place science-fair-winning destiny. "What's it to you?"

"It's an honor. A complete honor to me!" she exclaimed, shaking Wilmer's hand with such force that Wilmer thought his arm might be torn out of its socket and flung across the room. "How you saved the school . . . the pure scientific genius . . . wow! You're my hero!"

Wilmer was speechless. He hadn't expected *this* greeting.

"How does it feel to be the greatest kid scientist in the world?" she continued. "Do you feel different from normal kids? Does your brain weigh more?

The average human brain weighs three pounds, so yours must weight four or five pounds, right? Oh, what am I saying? Of course you haven't weighed your own brain! At least I hope not, because that would be impossible. Maybe I can weigh it for you? Of course I can't. Stop me. I don't know what I'm saying. You're so much handsomer in real life than I pictured. I don't know what I pictured. But you're smart and handsome and do you work out? You must. Look at those muscles. You're amazing."

Wilmer's jaw dropped. He had never been accused of having muscles before, and was pretty sure he didn't have any. He snuck a peek at Roxie. She looked at him and Harriet, frowning. But before he could ask what was wrong, Harriet jumped right into his line of sight, blocking his view, and then collapsed to the floor.

Wilmer gasped and quickly bent down. He put his hand under Harriet's prone head and lifted it gently. Her eyes were closed and she didn't move. "Harriet, are you all right?"

She opened her eyes and blinked. "I am now. Sorry. I'm just so overwhelmed by how amazing you are. The Amazing Wilmer Dooley. You must have girls faint around you all the time."

Wilmer shook his head. "Once I made my brother Sherman hiccup by sneaking up behind him, but I don't think that's the same thing."

Harriet laughed, a bit too loudly. "You're simply amazing, you Amazing Wilmer Dooley, you."

"Um, will you stop calling me 'amazing'?" asked Wilmer.

"Then I'll call you the Fantastically Perfect Wilmer Dooley."

"I think I liked 'amazing' better," said Wilmer, squirming.

Harriet burst out into a loud laugh. "And you're funny, too!"

"Sure, he's funny. Funny-looking," said Ernie with a chuckle. Wilmer scowled.

Roxie cleared her throat. "So. Anyway." She was still frowning at Harriet and Wilmer. "What do you guys think about the hotel? Have you noticed all the loudspeakers?" She pointed to the long line of speakers against the walls and ceilings. There were dozens. "I wonder if they have a broadcast room. Do you think they'll let me air my radio show here this weekend? Wouldn't that be awesome?"

Wilmer nodded enthusiastically until Harriet tapped him on the arm. "Forget about me?" she asked. Forgetting her would have been impossible, since she was now standing an inch away and on her tiptoes, staring up into Wilmer's eyes.

"I heard you won first place in some science award thingy," said Ernie to Harriet.

Harriet nodded and turned to Ernie, while still keeping one eye on Wilmer. "I won the Grand Newtonian in the national Newton Physics Awards. My Grand Newtonian project was on the power of sound, demonstrating how measuring sound frequency and amplitude can produce . . ."

Harriet stopped when she noticed Ernie staring blankly. "Sorry. You lost me at 'Newton,'" admitted a dazed Ernie. "But I really like Fig Newtons."

"Ernie's not really into science," explained Wilmer.

"Well, I can't blame him for being bored," said

Harriet. "Physics is *so* yesterday." She focused her full attention once again on Wilmer, gazing up into his nose from her short height. "Bacteria are *hot* right now. I simply love studying bacteria."

"Me too," said Wilmer.

"Oh, I know." Harriet sighed.

Wilmer looked away and noticed many of the kids around the lobby were watching him. He checked to see if his fly was unzipped.

Harriet leaned in. "They're staring because you're a star! Everyone has heard of *you*."

Two tall girls with curly, strawberry hair and thick glasses stood next to them. They appeared to be twins. Their shirts read, SCIENCE TECH PREPARATORY MIDDLE SCHOOL FOR PEOPLE WITH GIANT BRAINS. "Look, Tizzy," said one, frowning. "That's Wilmer Dooley. He doesn't look that tough."

Tizzy eyed Wilmer up and down, so that he felt like a lab mouse. "You're right, Lizzy. He doesn't look tough at all."

They both turned away with a sniff. Wilmer shrank.

"They're just jealous," Harriet whispered into

his ear, as if she could read his mind. "I think you're very tough-looking. But in a good way."

Wilmer coughed awkwardly. He didn't really want all this attention. But maybe—just maybe—Harriet was on to something. Wilmer *had* saved Mumpley Middle School, after all. It had been *his* genius that had found the cure to the plague. He *was* tough. Kids *should* be jealous of him.

Wilmer smoothed out his sweater vest, puffed out his chest just a smidgen, and stood a tiny bit taller. Ernie frowned at him. Roxie snarled. What was wrong with *them*?

"Let them envy you," whispered Harriet. "After all, you're the Amazing Wilmer Dooley."

Wilmer nodded.

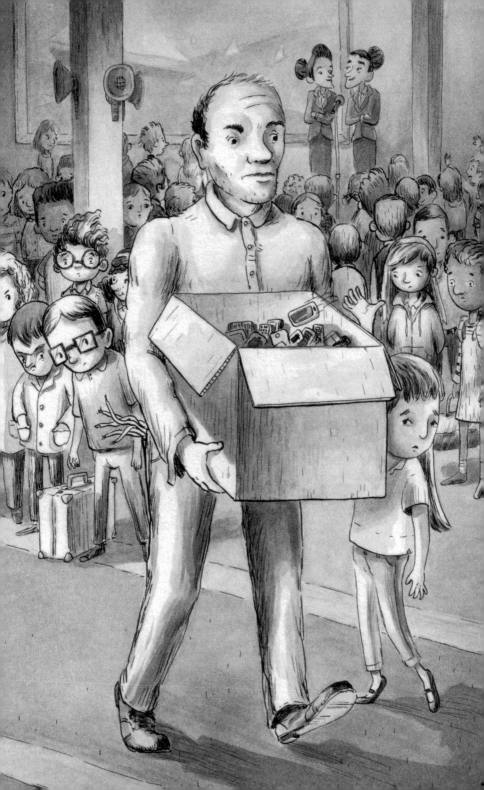

CHAPTER FIVE

To: _Wilmer Dooley_
Congratulations. You have been nominated by
Mrs. Valveeta Padgett
(it wasn't my idea, though)
to attend the 45th Annual State Science Fair
and Consortium,
the most prestigious and exclusive science
consortium in the state, for incoming seventh
graders only and some select sixth graders,
maybe.
August 6–8 at the
Sac à Puces Palladium, Lodge,
and Resortlike Hotel*.
By invitation only.
All electronic gadgets will be confiscated and
returned at the end of the weekend.

*New fancy-sounding location

The loudspeakers—all four dozen or so of them—
crackled. At first, Wilmer thought a canary was
screaming in his ear. Then he realized a speaker was

positioned only inches above his head. He covered his ears.

"Attention, dear, dear students," blared a voice, after an eerily off-tune screech. The man, or maybe it was a woman, sounded muffled and garbled and echoed, as if he or she spoke through a rag while eating a peanut butter sandwich inside a heating duct. Wilmer couldn't even be sure if it was an adult or a kid speaking. "Please make your way to the center of the lobby," boomed the unknown announcer. "Like good boys and girls. Like *very* good boys and girls." It was followed by a small chuckle, and then the speakers crackled one more time and went silent.

Wilmer rubbed his ears. Even though he had covered them, they hurt from the noise. The announcement had been so loud that it clouded his brain, but the feeling quickly subsided.

Luckily, Wilmer had earplugs in his pocket. It was one of the random science tools he carried with him at all times, like his empty test tube (courtesy of Mrs. Padgett's biology lab). A scientist was never sure when he would need to examine something carefully and in silence. He would be more prepared the next time those loudspeakers squawked.

Wilmer stepped forward and his friends followed. But where were Claudius and Vlad? They had been here a few moments ago.

They were probably lurking about somewhere. Claudius was a big-time lurker. Wilmer assumed Vlad was too.

Just up ahead in the middle of the lobby stood a tall, thin woman on a small raised platform. She wore a smart black business suit. Her hair was pulled back into a tight bun. Wilmer thought it was Valveeta Padgett, sixth-grade biology teacher and brand-new television personality. But no, it couldn't be, because his teacher stood next to the platform. Both women had their arms clasped, towering over the students.

"Welcome, my darling children," spoke the woman on the box. "I am Elvira Padgett, but please call me Elvira. Think of me as your friend, your best friend in the entire world. We can borrow each other's jeans, except I doubt we're the same size. I hope I can meet all of you, but it's a lot of work heading an entire science consortium weekend. I'm sure you can barely imagine the planning and so forth that's needed. Science sure is complicated, and I'm a hotel manager, not a scientist, so I know very little about sciency things. You kids sure are smart. I wonder how much your brains would weigh, if all weighed together."

Harriet turned to Wilmer. "I like her."

"So I am thrilled to welcome all of you, our future scientists, our best and brightest!" Elvira continued. "You should all be proud to be here. Bravo to you!"

Wilmer cheered along with the rest of the kids. He *was* proud to be there.

No. He *deserved* to be there. He *was* amazing, after all.

Harriet waddled closer to Wilmer. She had been approximately twenty millimeters from him before, but was now about ten millimeters away, or so Wilmer estimated.

"You're standing on my foot," he said. Harriet inched back another five millimeters.

Elvira looked around at the eager faces of her

audience, a sparkle in her eye. "I would also like to introduce Clarence Dillard Sneed, the caretaker of the hotel. Why, he loves children almost as much as I do!"

A tall, powerful but frazzled-looking man nodded from the side of the room. The few strands of his remaining hair were combed over his large, balding head. He wore a maintenance jumpsuit and held a large cardboard box. He grunted a raspy hello.

Elvira cleared her throat. "Mr. Sneed has been working very hard to get everything ready for the weekend and to keep the hotel in tip-top shape. Like me, he is here to serve you. Well, not actually *serve*. We're not tennis players. But we will do our best to make this a weekend none of you will ever forget. Although I bet most of you won't remember anything." She laughed, and so did Mr. Sneed, which struck Wilmer as odd. He hadn't heard anything funny.

"But I'm pleased as punch—and heaven knows punch can be very pleased with itself—to introduce someone else to you," Elvira continued. "Someone who needs no introduction, but whom I will introduce anyway. You all know her as the star of her own television show. I know her as my sister. May I welcome our special science fair judge: Valveeta Padgett."

Mrs. Padgett smiled—a tight, wincing smile—and waved. The kids cheered and clapped except for Wilmer and Ernie. Wilmer's stomach clenched. If she was the judge, winning the science fair wasn't going to be easy.

"Children, you'll notice Mr. Sneed has a box," Elvira continued. "As he makes his way around the room, please drop all your cell phones, cameras, games, tablets, headphones, and most especially, your iNoises inside. As you know, this is an electronics-free weekend. Be quick. You'll get them all back as good as new. Or even better." She laughed again, and so did Mr. Sneed. They certainly were two very happy people.

The kids in the crowd groaned as Mr. Sneed roamed around the room. Wilmer was the only kid in the entire hotel without any electronics to surrender.

Ernie plunged his iNoise into his back pocket and out of view. "You better give that to Mr. Sneed," said Wilmer.

"No way. A weekend without electronics is like a weekend without joy." Ernie shivered. "I feel so very cold."

"*I'm* not giving up my tape recorder or headphones," insisted Roxie, clutching her gadgets. "I'm a reporter, after all. Gwendolyn Bray wouldn't do it, that's for sure. I'm not even in the competition, anyway."

Mr. Sneed finished gathering the gadgets, although he didn't notice Roxie's or Ernie's. The oversize box looked very heavy, but the brawny hotel caregiver carted the box out of the room easily.

Wilmer also noticed loose wires sticking out of Mr. Sneed's back pocket. The poor man was probably busy all weekend laying cables, fixing lights, and doing other handyman jobs. It must take a lot of work to be the caretaker of an entire hotel.

Elvira rapped the microphone and its loud *pop pop* attracted everyone's attention once again. "We have a wonderful weekend planned. Tonight we will have a massive welcome feast, filled with foods you'll love. Tomorrow we have a whole menu of science activities to choose from, capped off by the famed Science Night Hike. It's a consortium tradition! Each of you will be dumped into the forest and you must find your way back to our lodge without being eaten by bears. Doesn't that sound like fun?"

A few kids, including Ernie, groaned, while others, such as Harriet, squealed with excitement.

Wilmer thought back to the drive to the hotel. His father had driven down a long and twisting dirt road, past cornfields and forests. The hotel was in the middle of nowhere. No, it was in the middle of the middle of nowhere. Getting lost in the woods at night was a distinct possibility.

But he *was* the Amazing Wilmer Dooley. He could do anything. Bears didn't frighten him. Much.

A fly buzzed by Elvira's head. She swatted at it.

"She seems very professional," said Roxie. "I'll need to interview her for my radio show."

Wilmer nodded, although with only tepid

enthusiasm. There was something about the woman that disturbed him. Maybe it was because she smiled just a little too brightly, or because she had just caught the bug buzzing around her head and was now tearing its wings off with a snort.

Wilmer scoffed at his overactive imagination. The fly probably had it coming.

Science, he knew, was based on observation, not imagination.

"And on Sunday," Elvira continued, "we will hold our world-famous science fair. I wish everyone could win. Why, then I'd give each of you a big squeeze, and then squeeze and squeeze like a boa constrictor!" She laughed. "Except an eighteen-foot boa constrictor can squeeze at approximately twelve pounds per square inch, and I could never generate that much force. But anyway, all of you are winners just for coming!"

The crowd cheered. Kids roared and clapped with enthusiasm. Wilmer just felt confused.

Ernie nudged Wilmer. "Why aren't you clapping with enthusiasm?"

"I thought Elvira said she wasn't a scientist,

but that boa constrictor fact sounded very scientific to me."

Ernie shrugged. "Maybe she just likes snakes."

Wilmer nodded, shrugged, and joined in on the applause. He needed to stop being so suspicious of people. He needed to focus on science and on the competition. Mostly on science. Like his dad said, he was here to learn!

But he couldn't completely lower his defenses. Claudius and Vlad had returned from wherever they had been lurking, and now they stood by Wilmer, giggling to each other. It wouldn't surprise Wilmer if they were planning something bad. The hairs on the back of his neck tingled. He inched forward a half step and leaned over, just close enough to overhear any evil whisperings.

There was plenty of time to learn science. Later.

"This weekend really *blows*," said Vlad.

This comment spurred a snicker and a nod from Claudius. "I bet science will *erupt* everywhere!"

Vlad nodded. "Oh, yes. The fair will be *spew-*

ing science." He laughed so loudly, spit flew from his mouth.

"What's going on, Wilmer?" asked Harriet, who leaned over alongside him.

"I'm not sure," said Wilmer, straightening. "At least not yet. But I'll find out. And if necessary, I'll save the day."

"Well, you *are* amazing," Harriet agreed.

CHAPTER SIX

Things to do this weekend:
- *Write and review scripts for Padgett!*
- *Sign autographs (it's so hard to be famous, but I can't let down my fans)*
- *Break in brand-new shoes*
- *Judge science fair (choose anyone but Wilmer Dooley)*

After the introduction from her sister, Valveeta Padgett basked in the claps and adulation of the children. She acknowledged their cheers with a mild half wave, like a princess might throw to a crowd of fawning peasants. "Thank you, thank you." After all, her show *Padgett!* was now the sixth most popular show on local access cable television, during her time slot on Sunday mornings.

But not everyone stared at her with admiration. A couple of kids glanced away, looking at . . .

Him! Wilmer Dooley! The rat. He threatened to steal some of her thunder, as he had done with those silly TV appearances and magazine articles throughout the summer. But anyone could have saved the school. He had been lucky, that was all.

His luck was going to run out this weekend if Mrs. Padgett had any say in the matter. And as the only judge of this science fair, she had plenty of say.

She rued his presence, knowing full well he wouldn't even be attending the fair if she hadn't nominated him. Principal Shropshire had insisted, saying that thousands of people were saved because of Wilmer and that twit, Ernie Rinehart.

Hardly! It had been *her* lab, *her* precious supply of cowitch powder, and *her* vats and burners that had saved the school. Wilmer Dooley was just a no-good credit-stealer, that's what he was. The school wasn't saved *because of* Wilmer Dooley, but *despite* Wilmer Dooley.

As she stood there secretly stewing, the loudspeaker went off, and Mrs. Padgett covered her ears. Her mind went fuzzy for a moment. The infernal PA system screeched like a million rusty hinges. This whole hotel was falling apart.

Mrs. Padgett looked at her sister, glowing and smiling at the crowd. She seemed to be enjoying herself. Surprising. Elvira had always hated children. Even as a child, Elvira disliked her classmates. She had changed quite a bit, which was probably for the best. Elvira was the black sheep of the family.

Wilmer spied Claudius and Vlad creeping off together, whispering and sneering. He considered following them. He could hide under that potted fern, dash behind the registration counter, and scamper up into the ceiling ducts. Or not. Ceiling ducts were full of dust and pollen, and Wilmer had allergies. Following them would also require quite a bit of slinking. And *amazing* people didn't slink.

Meanwhile, Harriet inched closer, which Wilmer didn't think possible. The top of her head was only about one hundred micrometers away from Wilmer's chin. Her eyes stared into his head like a fiber laser. Wilmer was forced to look away, fixating on the cracks lining the creaking walls and the water stains on the ceiling. This place was a dump, no doubt about it. But his ruminating was ruined when the loudspeaker over his head blared with a loud, ear-splitting squawk.

This time Wilmer was ready. He quickly blocked his ear canals with his earplugs. The other students were not so lucky. Many held their hands over their ears to lessen the horrible squealing noise.

Although his ears were plugged, the announcement was so loud Wilmer could still hear it. As before, the voice was so distorted that Wilmer wasn't sure who—or what—was talking.

"Attention, dear, dear students. We're just tidying up the exhibit hall and then you'll be able to set up your science fair projects. In the meantime, please go up to your rooms. We will call you down when we're ready. Don't forget to wash up! Always scrub behind your ears and between your toes. And your belly button."

Wilmer nodded. He always cleaned carefully behind his ears, scrubbed between his toes, and thoroughly lathered his belly button. He didn't need the reminder. But it was good advice, all the same.

Then the announcer gave what Wilmer thought was, just maybe, a sort of maniacal chuckle, and muttered the word "Fools!"

But through his earplugs, the electronic distortion, and the slightly numb feeling in his brain, Wilmer couldn't be certain of anything.

CHAPTER SEVEN

Dear Journal,

Ernie and I are relaxing in our room until we're called down. Ernie bounced on the bed when we came in, but he broke a couple of springs. And the TV doesn't work. And there's no room service. The phones are out too. And our window faces a brick wall.

Ernie also complained that his iNoise gets no reception, so he can only play a few games. The kid is seriously addicted to that thing. I don't know why anyone wants to play games when science is afoot!

It's more than afoot here, though. It's also a-leg and a-hip and a-spleen . . . an entire body of exciting scientific discoveries just waiting to be dissected.

This will be the best weekend ever. Or I'm not the Amazing Wilmer Dooley.

"Amazing." "Wilmer." Those words go together like "whooping" and "cough." "Chicken" and "pox." "Photo" and "synthesis"!

Wait. There goes the loudspeaker again. There's one right over the bed! I guess I'll be sleeping with my earplugs in. We're being called down to put our exhibits in the main showroom, have dinner, be kind to strangers, and hug a Canada goose.

It's a little strange that every announcement ends with a piece of good advice, but I guess it's helpful. I would never have thought to hug a Canada goose before now.

Scientific name: *Branta canadensis.*

I hope I can learn science all weekend. And win the science fair. And discover what Claudius and Vlad are up to. And get Ernie off that iNoise before his brain turns to jelly. That might be the hardest job of all.

Signing off,
(The Amazing) Wilmer Dooley

Wilmer dragged his enormous science project box into the exhibit hall while Ernie softly tossed his shoe box up and down. The room reminded Wilmer of his school cafeteria, except it was filled with many small tables rather than a few very long ones, and it lacked the smell of processed meat. A slight chalky taste of dust filled the air. As kids set up their projects all around him, the soft, invigorating hum of science made the small hairs on Wilmer's arms tingle.

Or maybe the hum was from the many oversize fluorescent light fixtures that hung from the ceiling and filled the room with a bright, flickering glow.

Wilmer found his name tag on a table. This is where he would set up his sure-to-be award-winning exhibit. Wilmer would need every inch of the table to fit his expansive project.

He opened his box and gazed at its contents with a gentle smile. He had spent weeks getting ready. Some nights his mother had brought dinner up to his room so he could continue working without interruption.

His room now smelled like asparagus-and-pickled-beet pasta with chicken gizzards, which had been last Thursday's disturbing supper.

But it was worth it. Wilmer felt confident. He still needed a couple of hours to arrange the banner stands, position the leeches *just so*, and ensure that the projector was set up with the perfect magnification and display. But then it would be first place–worthy.

Ernie's table sat directly next to Wilmer's. Ernie dropped his shoe box on it. "I'm done. No. Wait." Ernie opened the shoe box and stuck a wire into his potato. "*Now* I'm done."

"Not very impressive," said Wilmer.

"Maybe not," agreed Ernie. "But if I get hungry I can always eat my exhibit. Can you eat yours?"

Wilmer supposed he could eat the leeches if he was desperate. They probably didn't taste much worse than his mother's onion-coated garlic-gumbo balls. He still broke out in sweats at the mere thought of their oozy mashed-pea insides.

Scanning the room, Wilmer was impressed by many of the exhibits. The girls Lizzy and Tizzy were building what looked like a giant ant farm. One boy stood in front of a six-foot-tall pumpkin and a large sign about fertilizer. Another table featured a huge papier-mâché model of DNA spinning in a tall plastic tube.

Then Wilmer saw Harriet.

A few tables over, the sixth grader was setting up her project. It looked as grand as Wilmer's. Maybe even grander, he thought with a groan. Her exhibit actually looked very familiar. It featured retractable banners, a movie screen, a dozen glass vials, a jar of leeches . . .

"I did my project on contagions and the Mumpley plague," Harriet told Wilmer as he approached. "I've written a four-hundred-page book on bacteria, which I'm showing as a 3-D hologram. I have created a special breed of leech that sucks blood twice as fast. I have two electron microscopes to demonstrate bacteria at a molecular level. And I have a short movie starring Harvard's head of bacteriology discussing the principles of epidemics."

"But my exhibit is all about the Mumpley plague too," moaned Wilmer. *Only yours is better,* he thought.

"Oh, Wilmy!" exclaimed Harriet. "You're so

adorable! My exhibit can't compare to yours! True, I found a cure to the Mumpley malady that's more effective and cheaper to produce than yours, but *you* saved the town of Mumpley, not me."

Wilmer burned with jealousy, but he couldn't stay angry with Harriet. Not after she stumbled back and said, "Sorry. I can't help but swoon in your presence."

Across from Harriet stood Claudius and Vlad. A very tall black box sat on their table. They didn't open it. They just chuckled with malicious sneers.

"What's inside the box?" asked Wilmer.

"None of your business," barked Vlad. "But it'll blow the roof off this place."

Claudius chuckled. "Good one, Vlad."

"We'll have a *blast*," snickered Vlad.

"Boom!" added Claudius with a nearly hysterical guffaw. They both held their stomachs and rolled on the floor with hoots of laughter.

Wilmer's eyes narrowed into slits. Yes, they were up to something.

"And how is everyone doing today?" asked Dr. Dill. He strode quickly across the room. Vlad and Claudius stopped laughing and stood up. Vlad straightened his bow tie, and Dr. Dill delicately patted his nephew on the top of his head. "I'm so glad you came this weekend."

"What about me, Dad?" asked Claudius.

"You should be glad your cousin is here too." Dr. Dill patted Vlad until his Beethoven ringtone blared. "Oh, my special phone!" Dr. Dill exclaimed, answering it. "Dill here. . . . What? He's come down with Butter Fingers? We'd better make sure it doesn't spread. . . ." Wilmer didn't hear the rest of the conversation as Dr. Dill wandered away.

Claudius frowned, but then Vlad tapped him and whispered something in his ear, and the frown turned into a snarl—one aimed directly at Wilmer.

Wilmer was preparing to snarl back. It would be a tremendous snarl, possibly the most tremendous snarl of all time. When you were Wilmer Dooley— the Amazing Wilmer Dooley—you couldn't just give an everyday snarl, after all. But then Harriet grabbed his hand. It's hard to snarl while hand-holding.

"Do you mind?" she said, scooting closer.

"My hands are cold, and they warm three-point-five percent in your presence. Did you know that modern thermometers were invented in the early eighteenth century? Of course you do! You know everything!"

Wilmer hadn't known that, and he smiled awkwardly. He wanted to pull his hand away, but scientists need warm hands when handling delicate temperature-sensitive elements. It was his scientific duty to allow hers to heat.

"I was going to ask about your exhibit," said Roxie to Wilmer. He hadn't seen her approach, tape recorder in hand. "But I see you're busy."

"No, wait," said Wilmer, trying to release his hand from Harriet's, but her grip was too strong. Roxie stomped away. Wilmer watched as she melted into the crowd, interviewing other competitors. He wanted to chase after her.

But first, where were Claudius and Vlad? They had been standing right here a moment ago. They must have slinked away again. Probably off planning some horrible deed. Wilmer needed to be on his toes around them. Although it was hard for him to get up on his toes, since Harriet was standing on his foot.

He glanced at Claudius and Vlad's large unopened black box. Now was his chance. He could open it and peer inside. Maybe it hid a clue to their secret scheme! But touching someone else's science exhibit was against every science rule ever written, and a bunch more that should be written.

The loudspeaker squawked, removing any thoughts Wilmer had of box-peeking. In fact, for a moment it removed all his thoughts completely, scrubbing his mind clean like a whiteboard eraser. He had just enough sense to release Harriet's hand — she also seemed stunned by the noise — fumble for his earplugs, and thrust them into his ears as an announcement rang out.

"Attention, dear, dear students. Please make your way to dinner," said the voice, as muffled and unrecognizable as before. "And always sing happy songs to lost rabbits." A loud screech followed and the announcement was over.

Wilmer scratched his chin. He wasn't aware that lost rabbits liked to be sung to, but it was good to know. More importantly, it was time for dinner, and he was starving.

As he put his earplugs back in his pocket, Wilmer noticed many kids holding their ears from the deafening screech. Ernie was wincing— apparently he had very sensitive ears. "Are you okay?" Wilmer asked.

Ernie nodded, but slowly. "I think so. My brain feels a little fuzzy, that's all. It must be because I haven't played video games for so long."

"But you played with your iNoise twenty minutes ago."

Ernie shuddered with a look of pure horror. "Twenty minutes? It's a miracle I've lasted this long."

Wilmer's mind wandered back to the announcements. Ernie said his brain had been fuzzy. Wilmer had felt the same thing. Harriet was shaking her head as if to clear it. And where were Claudius and Vlad?

CHAPTER EIGHT

TONIGHT'S MENU:
WeinerBUZZZZ! hot dogs
Chili dogs
Corn dogs
Coney dogs
Yo, What-Up Dawgs
Chicken nuggets
Mac and cheese
French fries
Cheesy fries
Extra-cheesy fries
Extra-extra-cheesy fries with cheese
  dip
Chips (five kinds!)
Soda (twelve flavors ~~including one can
  of diet!~~)
Carrot sticks (three per table)
Candy bars, ice cream, cakes, giant
  mounds of sugar
Other things that are bad for you

Rows of long tables filled the dining room. On them
were giant wooden bowls crammed with glowing

yellow WeinerBUZZZZ! hot dogs, desserts, many other assorted bad-for-you-but-delicious foods and, all alone, a small dish with three carrot sticks. Kids filled their plates with near-hysteric excitement. Wilmer eyed the carrots.

Wilmer and Ernie hadn't even sat down and Ernie already had two hot dogs in his mouth. A bit of bun stuck out of his slightly glowing yellow lips, and breadcrumbs dotted his chin. Wilmer shook his head.

They grabbed empty seats at the end of a table. Roxie neared, and Wilmer dreamed she might sit next to him. He cleared this throat. He crossed his fingers and three toes in hope. He practiced saying, "Roxie, you look lovely," — but then Harriet hurried past and plopped herself down abruptly. "Mind if I sit here?"

"Well, actually—"

"Good." And that was that. Roxie sat across from Wilmer. She looked disappointed.

Harriet stared at the food on the table with a frown. "Processed meats. Salty foods. What I'd do for some spinach right now," she muttered.

"Really?" exclaimed Wilmer. "I like spinach too."

Harriet stared deeply into Wilmer's eyes. "I know."

Wilmer coughed and looked away. Had it suddenly become very warm in this room? "So. Roxie," he said after clearing his throat. "Are you going to give a special *Mumpley Musings* report this weekend?"

"I hope so. I looked for Mr. Sneed but couldn't find him. I'll need to track him down."

"Do you need any help?" Wilmer started to say, but he only got as far as "Do—" when Harriet grabbed his hand and squeezed.

"So! Wilmy!" she interrupted. "I love what you've done with your hair. What do you call that style anyway?"

"Um, moplike?" guessed Wilmer. He had never considered his hair anything but a disaster.

Harriet broke into a loud laugh. "Oh, Wilmy! You crack me up!"

Wilmer caught Roxie rolling her eyes. Maybe she was a little jealous? He smiled just a tiny bit.

He had never made any girl jealous before. He liked the feeling. Maybe Harriet's attention should be encouraged.

"Here's a funny joke," said Wilmer. He cleared his throat. He had read a series of jokes in one of his weekly science magazines and had memorized them, hoping to impress Roxie with his brilliant wit. "What did the glass slide say to the microscope?"

"I don't know," said Harriet, hanging on every word.

"Here's looking at you, kid."

Harriet broke into giggles. "Oh, stop! You're making my eyes water!" She wiped a stream of tears from her cheeks.

"That doesn't even make sense," snapped Roxie, staring at Harriet and folding her arms. "Why would a slide be looking at a microscope? The microscope should be the one saying the punch line."

Wilmer scratched his head. "Yeah, I think I reversed it. Sorry."

"Oh, no," said Harriet. "Your way is so much funnier."

A small grunt spilled from Roxie's mouth and a

satisfied grin broke over Wilmer's. Harriet beamed. Ernie was too busy stuffing his face with potato chips to pay attention to what anyone was saying.

To Wilmer's surprise, Vlad and Claudius sat down at their table. Vlad sat directly next to Roxie.

"We're supposed to sit with our schoolmates," explained Claudius, eyeing Wilmer. "Don't think we're sitting here because we like you."

"Where have you guys been?" asked Wilmer, his brain spinning with suspicion.

Vlad chuckled and pulled his earlobe. Claudius did the same.

Wilmer narrowed his eyes.

"I hear you're transferring to Mumpley this year," Roxie said to Vlad, shattering the silence like a dropped glass vial. She leaned toward him closely, a little too closely for Wilmer's taste. "Are you excited? Maybe we can hang out next year. You have a wonderful smirk. And I love your bow tie."

Now it was Wilmer's turn to be jealous. Vlad did *not* have a wonderful smirk. And bow ties were stupid. Why was she suddenly paying so much attention to him, anyway?

Roxie was now engrossed in full conversation with Claudius's cousin, nodding her head and smiling at everything he said. Fine, let her pay attention to him. Wilmer didn't need Roxie. He was *amazing*, after all.

"Aren't you going to eat?" asked Ernie, who was now on his fourth hot dog, or maybe his sixth.

"I guess so," said Wilmer, grabbing a carrot. But that wasn't going to fill him up. He knew vegetables are useful for improving the senses—carrots in particular have beta-carotene and vitamin A, both of which help to boost vision—but hot dogs have protein, and that's important too. Protein helps build muscle, fights against illnesses, and keeps nails strong, skin fresh, and bones healthy. Wilmer reluctantly grabbed a WeinerBUZZZZ!

As he chewed, Wilmer shuffled a little in his seat and felt a slight bulge in his pocket. He didn't remember putting anything in his pants. He reached in and pulled out what looked like a small Hershey's Kiss candy, except it was wrapped in orange foil. Attached to it was a small note:

Here's a special kiss for a special boy. Love, Mom

Ernie grabbed the candy out of his hand. "I'll take that, Wilmer-Poo," he said with a laugh. Before Wilmer could object, Ernie unwrapped the treat and flicked it into his mouth.

He immediately spit the candy on the ground. "Yech! What was that?" He chugged a large glass of glowing GrapeBUZZZZ! soda.

"One of my mom's tuna-oregano kisses with a splash of prune juice," said Wilmer with a shiver. "Don't worry. The taste should go away in a few hours."

Ernie quickly drank another glass of soda.

"Interesting." That's the word that popped into Mrs. Valveeta Padgett's mind as she surveyed the dining room. "Interesting," indeed.

She sat at a rectangular table on the side of the room. The table was on a slightly raised stage suitable for a guest of honor. It allowed her, Elvira, Dr. Dill, and some of the other chaperones to keep a watchful eye on the children. Not that Mrs. Padgett had an interest in watching children. At least, not usually.

Mr. Sneed's chair was empty—the man seemed to run around with wires in his pocket all the time. He must be busy fixing things. Mrs. Padgett looked at the walls and shook off the unsettling feeling that they were shifting. It seemed like a miracle that the entire building didn't collapse.

Still, that's not what was interesting, indeed. It was Wilmer and his crew that drew her attention. Claudius and his cousin had come in late, with mischievous snickers and furtive glances. If they were up to something, no doubt it would be bad news for Wilmer Dooley, which meant good news for Mrs. Padgett. She wished only the worst for him.

But Mrs. Padgett couldn't linger in the dining room for too long. She needed to finish her script for the next episode of *Padgett!* Her segment comparing mah-jongg dragon tiles to amoebas wasn't going to write itself (although even if it could, it would never write as well as Mrs. Padgett).

Elvira excused herself from the table and joined Mr. Sneed in the corner. They huddled. This had not been the first time Mrs. Padgett had spied her sister whispering with that man. They were way too cozy and secretive. Why, those two had been whispering in a closet yesterday! There was no reason to whisper in a closet unless it was a library closet and you were trying not to disturb librarians.

Throughout the room kids were talking loudly. Some yelled. Two boys threw French fries at each other! Mrs. Padgett stared, her eyes slits. If only kids were more like robots—subservient, trouble-free robots.

She ate the last of her tuna salad (specially requested and prepared just for her), anxious to get to work and away from the boisterous kids.

It was almost like school, but worse. At least school was over at 2:15 p.m. Here, there was no escape from them until Sunday.

Elvira returned to the table. "Kids can be quite uncontrollable," said Mrs. Padgett.

"If only we could find a way to control them."

Elvira flashed a surprisingly wicked grin. "To control them all."

Mrs. Padgett blinked. Now *this* was the Elvira she knew. Maybe she hadn't changed so much after all.

CHAPTER NINE

Mrs. Dooley's Five Worst Homemade Treats
A list by Wilmer Dooley

1. Prune sponges
2. Kidney-bean éclairs
3. Used-tennis-ball ice cream (with netting)
4. Sardine-flaked pastry cups
5. Jumbo pork-flavored, onion-infused cherry fizzes with fermented olive chunks

Wilmer and his friends finished eating. Ernie drank nine glasses of grape soda and still complained that the inside of his mouth tasted like tuna and oregano. Harriet laughed at twelve jokes from Wilmer, although she might have been faking it a little. Or maybe Wilmer was really funny. She nearly fell off the chair when Wilmer told this whopper:

"Why did the botanist agree with Carl Linnaeus's system of classification? He *hoped* he was right," which was an obscure joke based on famed eighteenth-century botanist John Hope. Harriet laughed so hard that some soda flew out of her nose and landed on Roxie's shirt.

Wilmer suspected that might not have been a total accident.

Despite the lavish attention Harriet paid him, Wilmer kept glancing at Roxie. He couldn't help it. She seemed awfully interested in Vlad, nodding as he talked, and staring at him like one gawks at a dividing amoeba. She complimented his bow tie. He showed her how to sneer. If only she would pay that much attention to Wilmer.

Instead, she entirely ignored him.

"Roxie, are you talking to a lot of kids about their exhibits?" asked Wilmer.

"Tell me more about your bow ties," said Roxie to Vlad.

Wilmer looked away, right at Harriet, who was staring at him and purring, "You are so amazing."

Across the table, Vlad abruptly scowled, tugged at his ear, whispered to Claudius, and stood up. Claudius scowled too, tugged his ear, and also leaped from his seat. They both scurried off without another word.

Where were they going? Was this part of their plan? Wilmer considered following them—he needed to learn more!—but then the loudspeaker squealed again. Wilmer's mind fogged. He had just enough sense to quickly plunge his earplugs in place.

The muffled voice from the speakers instructed the kids to go up to bed, since tomorrow would be a long day, "And be kind and friendly to earwigs."

"Who would ever be mean to an earwig?" asked Wilmer. He couldn't deny that it was good advice. Earwigs were friends to humans. They attacked mole crickets and chinch bugs, which were two nasty insects.

After the loudspeaker croaked out its final squawk, Wilmer put his earplugs safely back into his pocket. "We should go upstairs, Ernie."

Ernie stared at Wilmer blankly.

"Ernie? Hello? Earth to Ernie?"

Roxie also stared blankly. As did Harriet. Wilmer's heart jumped with worry. But then Roxie blinked. So did Harriet, and a moment later, Ernie blinked too.

"What's wrong?" asked Wilmer.

"What's wrong with what?" asked Ernie.

"You were staring blankly," said Wilmer.

"No, I wasn't," said Ernie. "But we should go upstairs."

"That's what I just said."

"No, you didn't. You're imagining things."

Wilmer didn't want to argue. Maybe Ernie was right. Claudius and Vlad had put him on edge, that was all. He just needed some rest. Everything was fine.

After Wilmer wished the group a good night, Harriet broke out in tears and cried, "I'll think of you every waking moment, and also my sleeping ones!"

Wilmer smiled awkwardly. As he rose to head upstairs, he noticed something bulging from his shirt pocket. He fished out a small peppermint-striped candy. A note from his mom was twisted around it:

For the sweetest boy I know!

Wilmer groaned. That was so like his mom. Although he was only gone for a weekend, she couldn't resist leaving him constant reminders of home. Mom needed to relax.

Before Wilmer could examine the candy more closely, Ernie snatched it away, tore off the wrapper, and popped it in his mouth.

"No, wait—" cautioned Wilmer.

Almost instantly Ernie gagged, spit out the candy, and moaned, "Water! I need water!" He sprinted away.

Wilmer picked the discarded sweet off the table and gave it a sniff. "Just like I thought," he remarked to Roxie and Harriet. "One of Mom's homemade five-alarm jalapeño-and-chili-powder jaw-droppers. Poor Ernie. Last time Mom made them, I had nightmares for weeks."

Upstairs, Ernie ran his pepper-inflamed tongue under the bathroom faucet while Wilmer sat on the bed, thinking of the wide expanse of lawn that surrounded the hotel, and the endless rows of trees beyond it. This was a strange location for a hotel. If anything went wrong, they were dozens of miles from civilization. The phones didn't work, Ernie's iNoise got no reception, and they were cut off from the rest of the world.

But what could go wrong? Wilmer was starting to worry, just like his mom. He laughed at himself. As long as Wilmer kept an eye on Claudius and Vlad, everything would go smoothly. At least, he hoped it would.

CHAPTER TEN

Dear Journal,

I can't help thinking of Ernie's blank stare at dinner, and Roxie and Harriet's equally empty gazes. But they probably don't mean anything. Nothing can get past me. I'm the greatest scientific observer I know!

Oh, wait, the notebook is upside down.

That's better.

People always say to trust your instincts. Bears instinctively know how to hibernate. Skunks instinctively know how to stink. And I instinctively know Claudius and Vlad are up to dirty tricks.

What are they plotting? My instincts can't tell me that.

But science is based on fact, not instinct. That's what separates scientists from bears and skunks. Well, that and fur and anal scent glands.

So what do I know, other than that Claudius and Vlad are hatching a twisted scheme to ruin everything?

I must look at the facts!

Fact: Vlad wears bow ties. I can't think of why that's evil. But maybe?

Fact: Claudius sneers quite a bit. Evil people sneer! Ergo, Claudius is evil!

Fact: They keep disappearing every time the loudspeaker goes off. Coincidence?

And what's with those messages, anyway? They're always ending with some piece of advice. Isn't that a little strange? Helpful, sure. But strange.

More importantly, what does Roxie see in Vlad? *I'm* amazing, not him! Harriet says I'm handsome and funny and that my teeth sparkle like pearls. She's really smart, so she must know what she's talking about.

If only Roxie could see how wonderful I am. She just needs to observe!

Like I do. Always.

Signing off,

(The Super-Amazing) Wilmer Dooley

At breakfast the next morning, Harriet pounced on the seat next to Wilmer. "Good morning, Wilmy," she sang.

Wilmer didn't look at her at first. He was too busy frowning at the piles of greasy bacon, dough-nuts, pancakes, and sausage patties on the table.

Oh, wait. He spied one grape tomato on a plate. He nabbed it.

"Did you sleep well?" asked Harriet, peering into Wilmer's eyes.

Wilmer nodded and blinked, surprised. "Harriet! Your hair is different. And I didn't know you wore glasses."

She wore round, thick, black-rimmed glasses that were almost exactly like Wilmer's. Her hair was messier—more moplike. Sort of like Wilmer's hair, actually. She wore a tan sweater vest that was remarkably similar to the one Wilmer often wore.

"Well, it never hurts to improve your vision," she said. "That's why I love spinach. It's packed with lutein and zeaxanthin, which help promote good eyesight."

"It also has folate and manganese, nutrients

that are good for brain function," added Wilmer.

"I could listen to you talk about spinach for hours," Harriet cooed.

Wilmer wiggled a bit uncomfortably in his chair. He looked away and scanned the room. Kids were calmer today than they had been the night before. Yesterday, students yelled and threw French fries, but now everyone was quiet, almost listless. Ernie especially seemed a bit slower than usual. He only had three sausages on his plate, and he picked at his doughnut with slightly less joy than Wilmer would have expected.

Claudius and Vlad, however, looked like their old selves. Vlad wore a big blue-and-yellow dotted bow tie. It's hard to look evil while wearing a bow tie, but somehow Vlad did. He and Claudius sat at the end of the table snickering. Occasionally they would stare about the room and tug their ears. Very suspicious. Then they would start giggling for no reason. But at this point, Wilmer would have been suspicious if they hadn't acted suspicious.

"Morning, guys," said Roxie, sitting down in the empty seat next to Vlad. Her earphones were draped around her neck and she carried her tape recorder. She smiled, casting a fleeting sunbeam of happiness at Wilmer. It almost cleared his head. He still felt slightly on edge despite a good night's rest. "Morning, Vlad," she said, directing her happiness beams away from Wilmer.

Wilmer was about to ask Roxie how her night had been, when Harriet tapped Wilmer on the shoulder and leaned in, blocking his view of everything but her head. "Last night I dreamed that $E=mc^2$, which of course represents Einstein's theory of relativity, was actually $m=Ec^2$. Have you ever heard of such a thing?" She laughed. "Of course you would never dream of anything so silly."

Wilmer had dreamed of a giant tap-dancing raisin, but he kept that to himself. Besides, he was only half listening despite Harriet's big intruding face. From the corner of his eye he could see Claudius and Vlad looking around and whispering to each other. "They are up to something," murmured Wilmer. "And *that's* a fact."

Harriet squinted at the cousins too. "You mean it's a theory, right, Wilmy? A theory is something you believe to be true but is not yet proven. A fact is something that can be shown beyond doubt. Such as the Jersey Giant being the largest breed of chicken."

"They weigh between eleven and thirteen pounds," added Wilmer. "But it's no theory. I have no doubt that Claudius and Vlad are up to sabotage. Cheating. Destroying stuff. I don't know *how*. Or *what*. Not yet, exactly. But I'm going to find out."

Harriet nodded. She stared at Claudius and Vlad with eyes as narrow and suspicious as Wilmer's. "If you say it's a fact, then it must be a fact. You are amazing, so you would know such things." She turned back to Wilmer, so close that her nose bumped his. "Excuse me," she said, but didn't move her nose, so it remained pressed against Wilmer's. "Can I help you solve this mystery? It would be a lifelong dream come true: working alongside Wilmer Dooley! Oh, look! My hands are shaking!"

Wilmer couldn't see her hands, since her head was in the way. But having a sidekick might be just the thing he needed to stop Claudius and Vlad from carrying out their mysterious plan. He couldn't have solved the contagious colors conundrum without Ernie and Roxie, after all.

Or maybe he could have. Yes, he probably would have done just fine by himself. He *was* amazing, just like everyone said.

Still, what harm could it do? "Sure, you can help. But can you move back a little? Your nose is crushing mine."

"Sorry! I didn't notice." She laughed and moved her nose five centimeters away.

"Morning, kids!" boomed Dr. Dill, strolling by. "Hello, Vlad and Clavicle!"

"That's Claudius, Dad."

"Right. Sorry. Good morning, Claudius Dad. And how is everyone else doing this morning?"

"Everything is—" began Roxie.

Dr. Dill's phone rang and he quickly answered it, leaving Roxie's mouth open, midsentence. "Dr. Dill here . . . What? She has Googly Eyes, you say? Don't let her out of your sight . . . !"

"He sure is busy," said Roxie, watching Dr. Dill rush off, still talking on the phone.

Wilmer nodded. "All great doctors are."

Claudius grunted.

Next to each of their plates was a sheet of paper. It listed all the science classes, workshops, and laboratory experiments kids could choose to participate in that morning. Harriet pointed to the seminar *Bacteria and Food: What's Eating You? Hopefully, Nothing.* Underneath the title it read: *A discussion and exploration of various food-borne bugs and how to prevent them.*

Wilmer nodded enthusiastically. That sounded like the perfect activity for him. He could barely believe his luck.

"Hey, Wilmer. We should do this," said Ernie, holding his sheet and tapping a class titled *How to Kick Butt in Video Games: A Discussion of Thumb Physics.*

Wilmer grimaced. He had promised Ernie they would hang out together. But keeping his word meant missing the bacteria discussion. Ernie looked at him with high hopes. Harriet tugged at Wilmer's arm and pointed emphatically to the food bacteria class. As Wilmer's brain churned, he overheard Vlad and Claudius.

"Let's take *Crystal Clear: A Beginner's Guide to Crystal Formations in Natural Habitats*," said Vlad. "It won't be as explosive as the rest of the weekend, though."

Claudius laughed. "Yes, explosive!"

Wilmer could think of few things more boring than making crystals. But he needed to keep an eye on those two. He announced, "I'm taking the crystal class."

"Are you sure, Wilmy?" asked Harriet with a small frown. "If you've seen one crystal, you've seen them all." But then she quickly added, "But yes! It'll be fun. Good idea. As long as we're together."

Ernie groaned. "That sounds like possibly the most awful class of all time. I'll stick with video games."

Wilmer glanced at Ernie. He felt a stab of guilt. Promises were promises. Best-friend thumbshakes were best-friend thumbshakes. But he needed to prevent whatever evil egg Claudius and Vlad were hatching.

In the front of the room, Elvira and Valveeta Padgett sat with Mr. Sneed. *Something* about

Elvira seemed off to Wilmer, but he couldn't place it. She was talking to a group of students, smiling and laughing and patting them on their heads with approval. "I love kids!" she gushed. She seemed perfect. *Too* perfect?

Wilmer shook his head. How could someone be *too* perfect? That would be like a single-celled amoeba being *too* single-celled. He was just paranoid because of Claudius and Vlad. They were clouding his judgment. *They* were the ones to watch. *They* were the reasons his suspicions were spinning around like an ultracentrifuge.

Mr. Sneed stood up from his chair and marched toward the door. As before, wires stuck out of his janitorial jumpsuit back pocket. That man's work must never be done, Wilmer thought, what with so many things in disrepair: the groaning walls, the water dripping from the ceilings and leaky pipes, and the hole in the lobby floor that Wilmer almost stepped in on the way to breakfast.

Roxie jumped from her chair. "There goes Mr. Sneed! I need to ask him about broadcasting my *Mumpley Musings* radio show at the hotel.

Maybe Elvira Padgett can be my first guest."

In her hurry, she left behind her headphones and tape recorder. Wilmer was about to shout after her when the loudspeaker squawked. Wilmer's mind went blank for a split second, but then he inserted his earplugs and his brain fuzziness cleared.

Harriet also put in earplugs. "I said to myself, if Wilmer Dooley can wear earplugs, then so can I!"

Wilmer glanced over to Claudius and Vlad. They were gone. Where had they snuck off to now? There was another loud squeal and the speakers buzzed with the usual odd half-human garbled voice.

"Attention, dear, dear students. Please make your way to your first activity. We hope you enjoy your day here at the Sac à Puces Palladium, Lodge, and Resortlike Hotel. And always build igloos for down-on-their-luck polar bears. Thank you."

"The poor down-on-their-luck polar bears," said Wilmer with a nod, removing his earplugs. "Right, Ernie?"

Ernie gazed off into space. The girl next to Ernie did the same and so did the boy next to her, and the boy next to him, and so on down the line. In fact, just about every kid seemed to be spacing out. There were a few exceptions: a girl with a giant mop of frizzy hair so large you could barely see her face; a small boy who seemed to wear earmuffs all the time (Wilmer had overheard him complain about having cold ears); and a large bug-eyed kid who wore a winter hat pulled tightly over his head. They continued to eat breakfast as if nothing had happened.

Harriet also looked normal. Wilmer leaned over to her. "Have you noticed kids acting weird?" he asked.

She shook her head. "What do you mean?"

"Kids are spacing out and I don't know why."

Harriet shrugged. "Are you sure?"

"Of course I am. And Claudius and Vlad keep disappearing. I bet it's all connected somehow."

"I don't know, Wilmy. Claudius and Vlad are probably just off somewhere talking about science."

"Yes, but good science . . . or evil science?" wondered Wilmer.

"You worry too much. I'm sure their vanishing has nothing to do with anything. It's just a big coincidence."

Wilmer frowned. There were no such things as coincidences.

Well, there were, sometimes. Take Buzz Aldrin, the famous astronaut. He was the second man to ever walk on the moon. His mother's maiden name was Moon. A pretty cool coincidence. Or the strange case of Hugh Williams. It's rumored that in 1660, a ship sank in the English Channel. The only survivor was named Hugh Williams. In 1767, another ship supposedly sank in the same place and had only one survivor. He was also named Hugh Williams. In 1820, another boat sank in English waters. The only survivor was named Hugh Williams. In 1940, another British boat sank and had only one survivor. Yep, his name was Hugh Williams too.

But *this* was no coincidence! If something walks like a duck and quacks like a duck, it's a duck. Unless someone is wearing a duck costume for Halloween, or is a confused chicken. "A true scientist can always tell the difference between coincidence and fact," declared Wilmer.

Harriet nodded. "We'll need to keep our eyes open, then. The *Amazing* Wilmer Dooley is never wrong."

"What are you two whispering about?" asked Ernie, who, along with the rest of the kids in the room, had apparently snapped out of his trance.

"Do you feel different?" asked Wilmer. "Odd? Blanker? I think Vlad and Claudius might be up to something. Something bad."

"What are you talking about?" asked Ernie.

"You keep zoning out," explained Wilmer.

Ernie rolled his eyes. "That's ridiculous."

"Be careful about eye rolling, it could strain your ciliary muscle," cautioned Wilmer.

A boy with a lime-green winter hat pulled over his head shuffled casually past them. Wilmer recognized him as one of the few students who had been acting normally. Wilmer jumped up and blocked his way.

"Hey. You. During breakfast, did you notice anything odd?"

"What?" the boy asked.

"Everyone seemed to be staring blankly."

"What?"

"Kids were gazing into space at breakfast."

"What?" The kid pulled off his hat. "Sorry, I can't hear a thing with this hat on. What did you say?"

"Never mind." Wilmer sighed.

Something *was* going on. Wilmer just didn't know what. Yet.

CHAPTER ELEVEN

SCIENCE FAIR ELECTIVE 4-C

*Crystal Clear: A Beginner's Guide to Crystal
                    Formations in Natural Habitats*

*Saturday 10:00 a.m., The Wolverine Suite
    Taught by Dr. Fernando Dill, the World's
    Greatest Doctor*

Crystallization is one of the most
elementary processes of chemistry; a
fundamental procedure that all chemists
must master. In nature, examples of
crystallization include stalactites and
stalagmites, as well as gemstones and—
Sorry, I need to take this phone call.

*Crystal Clear: A Beginner's Guide to Crystal
Formations in Natural Habitats* was held in the
Wolverine Suite on the opposite end of the lobby.
It must have been named after the set of stuffed
wolverines hanging from the wall. They stared
out, their jaws set in mid-howl. It was disturbing.
Wilmer tried not to look at them. Instead, he focused

on the microscopes, thermometers, Bunsen burners, test tubes, and safety goggles on each table,
along with sodium thiosulfate and other chemicals
in vials. Wilmer and Harriet entered the room but
waited to grab their spot until after Claudius and
Vlad had arrived. The two cousins nabbed the table
at the very back corner, and Wilmer and Harriet
snagged the one right next to them. Wilmer had to
cut off the twins Lizzy and Tizzy, who tried to grab
it first.

Soon Dr. Dill strolled in and stood in the front
of the class.

"Welcome, students," said Dr. Dill. "Today you
are going to form crystals and . . ." His Beethoven
ringtone interrupted him. "Excuse me!" He fished
his phone from his pocket. "Dill here . . . What? . . . He
has Tongue Twisters? . . . Yes, they could be caused
from eating pickled peppers. . . ." Phone pressed
against his ear, Dr. Dill dashed out of the room.

The kids stood, uncertain what to do. Fortu-
nately, a set of instructions was at each table. Every
pair of scientists needed to heat the chemicals in a
tube, seal it, let it cool, and then add sodium thio-

sulfate. Clear crystals would soon form. The students got to work.

It seemed pretty easy, so Wilmer only needed to pay a little bit of attention to his project and focus *most* of his attention on Claudius and Vlad. The two cousins rotated between being very quiet, pulling their ears, giggling, and whispering to each other.

Wilmer tried to listen in on their whispers. Luckily, he had used earplugs during the hotel announcements, so his razor-sharp hearing was still in pristine condition. Who knows what tiny ear hairs might have wilted if abused by the scratchy loudspeaker rumblings?

"It'll blow, right?" mumbled Claudius.

"Of course," Vlad whispered back. "The biggest eruption you've ever seen. I can't wait to see the look on everyone's faces."

"I can just imagine Wilmer's blank face as he is engulfed in . . ."

Blank face! Engulfed in . . . what? Wilmer inched closer. Their voices dipped even lower, so he couldn't quite make out what they were saying. He wiggled toward them.

". . . their hopes crushed like a pureed tomato."

"Like a smashed and minced pureed tomato. That's seeded."

Wilmer leaned over to hear.

"As long as we're far enough away when it's ignited," mumbled Claudius.

"And if things get destroyed?"

"We can only hope so."

"So the plan is . . ."

Wilmer leaned over even more.

Uh-oh.

He had inched a bit too close. Wilmer hadn't realized that he was leaning over their table, leaning so far that he lost his balance. He waved his arms to keep steady, and accidentally swiped Claudius's and Vlad's experiment across the table and onto the floor.

KCRZZZIGLE!

Test tubes shattered. The Bunsen burner flew onto the floor and broke in half, its flame extinguished. Chemicals spilled. Wilmer forced a half-hearted, embarrassed smile, and then realized that every kid in the room was glaring at him.

"Um, sorry?" mumbled Wilmer. He felt like he was turning as red as a StrawberryBUZZZZ! Popsicle.

"What do you think you're doing?" snarled Claudius.

The other kids began growling, and two barked like dogs.

Wilmer gulped. The students' fuming stares pierced him like toothpicks, poking and jabbing him with rage.

Wilmer took a small step backward. The reaction from the kids surprised him. Sure, he had just ruined the cousins' project, which was a serious violation of the scientific code of honor. But it was an accident! And scientists were usually slow to anger.

Jealousy.

That explained it. When you're at the top, people are always looking to drag you down. And the Amazing Wilmer Dooley had so very far to fall.

Wilmer took another step backward. The other students moved toward him. Where was Dr. Dill when you needed him? "But they're up to something!" Wilmer pointed to Claudius and Vlad.

"They're going to blow up the hotel or something horrible!"

"A scientist needs proof," spat Lizzy, cracking her knuckles.

"A scientist needs facts," hissed Tizzy, jabbing a pencil.

"He has neither!" roared Vlad. "He's just desperate for attention. Like always."

"He's been this way ever since the Mumpley contagion!" shouted Claudius. "He's always walking around like he's better than everyone!"

Wilmer slumped back another step. He gasped for breath; the stares in the room were suffocating him. "But I-I do know stuff," insisted Wilmer. "I know these two." He pointed to Claudius and Vlad. "They've been whispering."

"Oh. We've been whispering!" said Vlad in mock horror. "Call the police!"

"Lock up the librarians!" yelled Claudius. "They whisper too!"

"And hoarse people," said Vlad. "Hoarse whisperers."

"No, it's not like that," moaned Wilmer, inching back even more. Unfortunately, he bumped into his own table, knocking over his vials and tubes. They smashed on the floor too.

"And now he's destroying that girl's stuff!" screamed a tall boy in a lab coat, pointing to Harriet.

"Actually, that's my stuff," croaked Wilmer.

"He's a fake," said Claudius, pointing at Wilmer. "A vicious fraud! He didn't find the cure to the Mumpley malady last year. I did!"

"You did not!" protested Wilmer.

"Who are you going to believe?" Claudius asked the kids in the room. "Me, or the guy who just smashed all my stuff for no reason?"

"But he *did* cure the school," whispered Harriet, her voice cracking. "Didn't you, Wilmy?" Her eyes watered.

"Everyone settle down," pleaded Wilmer as the students neared. "Everything's okay."

"It's not okay with me," snarled Lizzy.

"And it's not okay with me," stormed Tizzy, thwacking a ruler against her leg.

Wilmer took three steps closer to the door. "But I *did* find the cure. Knocking over their stuff *was* an accident. Claudius and Vlad *are* hatching some horrible plan. I know it!"

The kids in the room stomped forward. These weren't normal, everyday scientists. They were scientists thirsty for blood. Wilmer's blood!

A crackle announced that the loudspeakers were about to blare. The other students came to an abrupt halt. Wilmer pushed in his earplugs just before the distorted voice shot across the room. Harriet put hers in too. Claudius and Vlad tugged their ears.

"Attention, dear, dear students," rang the eerie, altered voice. "We hope everyone is enjoying their activities. Just remember to donate your birthday gifts to charity, and mice need love too!" And the announcement ended with a squeak.

"I always donate gifts," said Wilmer, "but I'm not sure about loving mice, to be honest."

No one moved. A few kids dribbled spit from their mouths. Everyone wore vacant expressions, almost as if their brains had been emptied and needed to be refilled. Everyone, that is, but Claudius, Vlad, Harriet, and Wilmer.

"Tell me it isn't true, Wilmy," Harriet muttered. "Tell me you're not a fraud."

"I'm not! It's them!" Wilmer yelped, pointing to Claudius and Vlad. "They're the troublemakers."

And I'm amazing! They'll pay for doubting me!

Wilmer blinked. Now why did he think *that*?

Some kids were now blinking too, losing their empty looks. They appeared even angrier, if that was possible—their brows were furrowed, their foreheads crinkled with fury, their fingers curling into fists.

Claudius screamed, "Down with the fake! Down with Dooley!"

Wilmer, backing up, smashed into Dr. Dill, who was walking back into the room, still on his phone. "A serious case of Fanny Packs? Horrors! You need to grab . . . Oomph." Dr. Dill dropped his phone when Wilmer collided with him.

"Er, sorry," said Wilmer.

Dr. Dill leaned over to pick up his phone. Wilmer sidestepped him and dashed out the door.

CHAPTER TWELVE

Dear Journal,
   Everyone's supposed to attend a brief seminar about the Science Night Hike, but I'm not going. I can't face anyone after this morning's disaster. I wonder if I can just hide here in my hotel room the rest of the weekend, like an ostrich with its head in the sand.
   Ostrich: *Struthio camelus*
   But why should I? I'm no ostrich! Let them all hide their heads from me! How dare no one believe me! Let Claudius and Vlad blow up the hotel or carry out whatever scheme they've crafted. It would serve everyone right.
   What am I thinking?
   I'm thinking I'm better than everyone else.
   No, I'm not.
   Yes, I am.

No, I'm not.

Well, it doesn't matter. They'll all come groveling to me when they see I was right and they were wrong.

No, they won't.

Yes, they will.

What's going on? My brain feels like it's swirling with dust clouds. A scientist must be clearheaded. A doctor must be that way too! I'll need to concentrate harder on staying alert.

No, I won't.

Signing off,

Wilmer Dooley

At lunchtime Wilmer finally went downstairs, his stomach murmuring with hunger, but tingling with a mix of rage and self-pity.

As he sat down in the cafeteria, he didn't see Claudius or Vlad. Like usual, they were probably off somewhere lurking.

Wilmer grabbed a slice of pizza and soaked up some of the grease with his napkin. He missed his creamed spinach—its healthy assortment of vitamins would make him feel better.

Harriet sat next to Wilmer. She put her hands on his shoulder and leaned in, smiling. Her hair looked even more moppish than it had earlier. "After you left the workshop, I made some spectacular crystals. How are you?"

"Leave me alone," grumbled Wilmer.

Harriet looked down, her eyes watering. "Wilmy, I'm sorry I doubted you. I don't know what I was thinking. Something came over me. I haven't been myself. Can you forgive me?" She clutched his arm and gazed with pleading eyes. "Please?"

Wilmer nodded. He knew exactly what she meant because he didn't feel like himself either. It was as if a small kernel of outrage remained lodged in his brain.

Ernie sat on the other side of Wilmer. He was quiet and seemed distracted. He picked up the pizza on his plate and gnawed at the crust.

"How was your video game class?" Wilmer asked.

Ernie didn't respond.

"Ernie? Hello?" repeated Wilmer.

"What?" said Ernie, as if emerging from a fog.

"I was asking about your class," repeated Wilmer.

"We did thumb exercises," said Ernie, flexing his thumb up and down and up. "I'm ready for video games and hitchhiking." For good measure, he added, "As if you care." *He* seemed on edge too.

"I do—" *Care*, is what Wilmer meant to say, but he was interrupted by a brief announcement from the loudspeaker. Wilmer's brain momentarily clouded as he fumbled for his earplugs. He inserted them into his ears just before the speaker spoke. Harriet put her earplugs in too.

"Attention, dear, dear students. Enjoy your meal, and always use an umbrella—a dry day is a happy day!" That was the entire announcement.

Wilmer popped out his plugs. "I do like dry days. Rainy days make me angry!" He snarled, and then gasped at his unprovoked fury. He took a deep breath. "What do you think, Ernie? Ernie?"

Ernie stared forward without blinking. So did most of the kids in the room.

Wilmer looked at Harriet. Harriet looked back at him.

"What are you looking at?" Wilmer grumbled.

"What's it to you?" she growled.

Then, just as suddenly as it began, the group trance ended. Kids began to eat again. Wilmer took a deep breath. Where had that anger come from?

"Sorry," he said to Harriet, remembering his harsh words.

"I'm sorry too," she said, with meaning.

"Look, there's Wilmer Dooley," muttered Lizzy, walking behind him. "Claudius Dill told me that Dooley takes credit for other people's work because he's so full of himself."

"That makes me so mad," said Tizzy. "And Claudius Dill told *me* . . ."

Wilmer didn't hear the rest of their conversation as they receded into the crowd. But it wasn't true! People are only full of themselves if they think they're great and they aren't. Wilmer *was* great, so he was just being honest about himself.

How dare they doubt me!

Wilmer shook his head, trying to clear the outrage from his brain. What was going on with him?

Roxie sat down across the table. She wasn't

wearing her earphones and didn't have her tape recorder with her.

"Hey, Roxie," said Wilmer. "Did you speak with Mr. Sneed or Elvira about the radio show?"

"Yes, and I'm not giving my show, okay?" she said with a grunt. "Are you happy now? Just leave me alone."

Wilmer bit his lip. Roxie's harsh words were more hurtful than everyone else's comments put together. "I don't like this," Wilmer whispered to Harriet. "I just wish I knew Claudius and Vlad's plan. Do you think it has something to do with the loudspeakers? Have you noticed how everyone stares blankly after each announcement? And everyone seems angry. I'm angry! And it's getting worse."

"That's a dumb idea," muttered Harriet. She gasped. "Did I just say that? Maybe you're right. Maybe there is a connection. I just don't see how Claudius and Vlad could possibly—"

"It's Claudius and Vlad," insisted Wilmer, with conviction. "They're making these announcements."

And they'll be sorry they messed with me!

"But didn't an announcement go off during the crystals workshop?" asked Harriet. "They were standing right near us."

"I'm always right!" screamed Wilmer. He gasped at the harsh sound of his voice. "I didn't say they weren't clever," he continued, taking a deep breath. "Maybe they played a prerecorded message. Or they're ventriloquists. That's it! Vlad is the ventriloquist and Claudius is the dummy." He snorted. "But they can't fool me. Science is about persistence and forcing your opinions on others."

"But I thought science was about observation," said Harriet. "You said—"

"Forget what I said. Claudius and Vlad are guilty. They'd do anything to win this science fair, even if it means fogging everyone's brains and blowing things up."

"You know best, Wilmy. As you say, Vlad and Claudius have been planning this for months. They've somehow rigged up an elaborate loudspeaker system and are doing something for some reason so they can win the science fair or maybe explode things." She nodded her head. "That makes complete sense. The Amazing Wilmer Dooley has done it again."

The loudspeaker chose that precise time to squawk. This was Wilmer's chance to be a hero! He'd show them all just how amazing he was. He jumped out of this seat. "Quick! Everyone cover your ears!" he shouted while putting in his earplugs.

Kids looked at Wilmer like he had lost quite a few marbles and they were rolling all over the ground. Some shot him dirty looks. Many sneered and hissed at him.

No one covered his or her ears.

"Hurry!" Wilmer demanded. "The loudspeakers are making your brains fuzzy! Save yourselves!"

No one tried to save anyone.

"Attention, dear, dear students," rang the garbled voice on the loudspeaker. "We hope you've enjoyed lunch. Please head to your afternoon activity. And hug a dolphin. And remember that a clean cuticle is a happy cuticle." This was followed by a cackle—maybe a maniacal one, it was hard to tell with all the distortion—and then another loud chirp and then silence. Ernie and Roxie stared forward, drool dripping from their chins. Throughout the room many kids stared, some with their tongues hanging out.

Dr. Dill walked past. He didn't stare or drool. In fact, he acted completely normal. Was *he* behind whatever was going on? He *was* Claudius's father. Evil *could* run in the family.

Dr. Dill is guilty! He's rotten to the core! I must stop him!

Wilmer tightened his fists so hard his knuckles turned white. He took a deep breath. He needed to get a grip. Dr. Dill couldn't be like that. He was the World's Greatest Doctor. Doctors swore to help others, not to hurt them. Wilmer needed to get his anger under control. "Dr. Dill!" shouted Wilmer, swallowing a growl. "Help! The loudspeakers are making kids space out and drool!"

"Drool? Why, that's horrible!" agreed Dr. Dill. "We should do something!" The music of Beethoven trickled from his pants pocket. He quickly dug out his phone and answered it. "This is Dr. Dill, I can't talk and . . . What? An epidemic of Borscht Belt? Are you joking . . . ?" He hurried out without another word to Wilmer.

Wilmer felt like jumping up and tackling the doctor. He needed his help.

But then Roxie blinked, as did Ernie. Slowly, all the kids began to move again. Wilmer felt relieved, and his anger died down just a bit too.

"Are you okay?" Wilmer asked Ernie.

Ernie growled at Wilmer.

Harriet leaned close to Wilmer and slipped her arm around his. "I still think you're amazing." Suddenly, she snarled. "And the thought of anyone thinking differently makes me so mad I just want to tear their hair out!"

Ernie held up the menu of activities and jabbed his finger at a class on building miniature rocket ships. "Class is starting," he snapped. "Are you coming?"

Before Wilmer could respond, Harriet squeezed his hand and yanked him out of his chair. "Wilmer and I have more important things to do," she said. "There's a class on scientific love potions that looks perfect."

"Love potions?" asked Wilmer with a gulp.

"Let's go," said Harriet, roughly pulling Wilmer behind her. "If we hurry we can get good seats."

"But—" began Wilmer.

Harriet gnashed her teeth. "I said we're going to love potions. Don't mess with me!"

"I'll see you later, Ernie, okay?" shouted Wilmer. "Ernie?"

Ernie stomped away while Harriet pushed Wilmer toward the door.

CHAPTER THIRTEEN

Dear Journal,

I'm glad I brought you to class. I need something to distract me. It's pretty crowded here in the love potions workshop. The room is filled with three dozen girls and me. I guess girl scientists are much more interested in love than guy scientists. At least in middle school.

You'd think everyone would be all lovey-dovey in a love potions class, but no. Harriet is snarling at me. Most of the girls are arguing with each other. Lizzy just stomped on my foot.

The workshop started with a discussion about pheromones. Those are chemicals that animals secrete to attract mates. Male cockroaches are loaded with them. Rodents, too. Harriet seemed really interested and took a lot of notes, but I'm not sure why she would want to attract cockroaches or mice. We also learned about online mah-jongg.

Oh yeah, Mrs. Padgett is teaching the class. Twice she's told me to be quiet, but I haven't said a word. I guess I'm writing too loudly.

I should be spying on Claudius and Vlad and not wasting time in here. They could be up to anything, anywhere.

But without proof of their evil plot, I'll just be ignored again, especially since Claudius has been telling everyone I'm a fraud. People believe what they want to believe, I guess.

I have to admit, arranging an elaborate loud-speaker system to cloud two hundred middle-school scientists' brains seems like a lot of work just to win a science fair, even one as prestigious as this. But I know better than to put anything past Claudius. If he put half as much energy into science as he does into sneaking and plotting, he might actually do some good.

Ow! Harriet is nudging me. No, she's plucked a hair from my head. Maybe this next potion needs a human hair. I better start paying attention.

Maybe I can learn a few things and slip a love

potion to Roxie. My heart still belongs to her, even if she can barely stand me anymore. If only I had called her this summer like I promised! If only I wasn't such a wimp!

An amazing wimp, though.

Ow, again. Harriet just pinched me. No, she grabbed a piece of dead skin and is putting it into a beaker. I'd better go.

Signing off,
Wilmer Dooley

During dinner there was only one loudspeaker announcement, and Wilmer and Harriet popped in their earplugs as the horribly familiar wave of disturbing blankness spread over the room. Wilmer felt a surge of anger, but he managed to keep it from frothing out.

The empty stares lasted longer this time. Ernie was completely vacant for one minute and twenty-two seconds, according to Wilmer's estimate. Again, Claudius and Vlad were nowhere to be seen.

Roxie wore her headphones and was fiddling with her tape recorder the whole time. Good. If the loudspeakers were rigged, as Wilmer suspected, then her headphones had likely protected her.

But soon the kids in the room began acting normal again. Well, *somewhat* normal. Wilmer heard arguments erupt from tables. A small fight broke out.

"Dear children, are you excited for the night hike?" Elvira asked Wilmer and his friends. She had been walking around, cheerfully chatting with the students. Wilmer nearly fell off his seat in surprise; he hadn't seen her behind him.

"Sure," said Wilmer, spinning around on his chair. "But have you noticed everyone's angry?"

She giggled. "Oh, I'm sure they're just nervous about the fair. Competition can make people cranky. Studies show that stress can decrease serotonin levels, which increases crankiness. But I'm a hotel manager, not a scientist, so what do I know?"

"But it seems to go beyond just crankiness...." insisted Wilmer.

"Nonsense!" Elvira interrupted, smiling.

"But—" continued Wilmer.

"She said it's just competition crankiness!" growled Ernie.

"But then why are you cranky?" asked Wilmer. "You don't want to win."

"Because I can't win? Is that what you think?" challenged Ernie.

"No, it's just that—"

"Arguing kids are so cute!" Elvira giggled. "Well, good luck tonight. I hope a bear doesn't eat you!" She turned to chat with the kids seated at the next table over.

Ernie glared at Wilmer. Wilmer hoped the fresh air of the night hike might clear his best friend's head. And his own head, too.

"Darling students, please go to the front of the hotel for the night hike!" announced Elvira. "I love you all!"

Everyone began to push and bang their way out of the cafeteria. Ernie grabbed a cupcake and crammed it into his jacket pocket. It was a glowing orange Marmalade ChocoBUZZZZ! cupcake—one of Wilmer's dad's most popular sellers. "In case I get hungry," he muttered. "And you can't have any!" he added with a snarl to Wilmer.

They were split into small groups. Wilmer was teamed with the Mumpley kids: Ernie, Harriet, Roxie, Claudius, and Vlad. Good. The cousins couldn't do much mischief under Wilmer's observant eyes. He could keep an eye on Ernie, too; his friend seemed more irritable than anyone else.

The team was also assigned two chaperones: Dr. Dill and Mrs. Padgett.

They all rode in the back of a truck driven by Mr. Sneed. Wilmer couldn't see a thing. He was blindfolded, as were the other students.

"I wish we had seat cushions," said Wilmer. He sat on a hard wooden bench, and every time the truck bounced and jostled, it felt like someone was hitting him with a paddle.

"Stop whining," groused Ernie.

"Remember," said Mrs. Padgett, "we will drop you off in the middle of the woods and you'll have to find your way back using science and navigation skills."

"Can we get our iNoises back?" asked Claudius.

"They come with a GPS navigation system."

"Absolutely not," said Mrs. Padgett. "Besides, you'd get no reception out here."

"What if we can't find our way back? Or get attacked by bears?" asked Roxie.

"That's why you have chaperones," explained Mrs. Padgett. "Not that I'll be going. I could scuff up my brand-new shoes. A night hike! Who would have imagined! But you'll have Dr. Dill to help you. Right, doctor? Doctor?"

Wilmer heard Dr. Dill's familiar ringtone followed by his booming voice. "This is Dill . . . Yes? . . . He has Elbow Grease? Have you tried cleaning it? . . . Well, scrub harder, man!"

There was a big thud, the truck leaped, Wilmer flew up a good six inches before crashing back down on the hard seat, and then the truck stood still.

"We're here," said Mrs. Padgett. "You may remove your blindfolds."

They were deep in the forest. With the thick tree branches blotting out the night sky, it was almost completely black. They could be practically anywhere.

The kids carefully stepped down from the truck bed one at a time. Wilmer's eyes soon adjusted to the dark. But it was still almost impossible to see more than a few feet in front of him.

"Good luck," said Mrs. Padgett as the truck pulled away.

"Wait! Is Dr. Dill coming?" asked Ernie.

"A rare case of Bell Bottoms has flared up? Say it isn't so!" Dr. Dill screamed into his phone from the truck.

"Just head north!" Mrs. Padgett hollered as the truck vanished into the night.

The kids were alone and lost. A chilled air cut through their bones. Who knew how far they were from the hotel? And which way was north?

The forest was silent except for the sound of a single cricket. *Chirp. Chirp.*

And maybe a snake? And a bear. Definitely a bear.

Wilmer stiffened. He wasn't afraid of the dark. Not really. Seventh-graders-to-be were too old to be afraid of the dark. Still, he didn't feel entirely *not* afraid, either. Truth be told, Wilmer was most at home in front of a microscope or reading a medical book, not lost in the wild. He'd have to act brave anyway. He couldn't show Roxie, or any of them, that he was worried.

I won't give them the satisfaction!

Wilmer shook his head. The night air was helping him simmer down, but not completely. He needed to try harder. "Isn't this fun?" Wilmer said bravely. No one answered right away.

"No, it's not fun," snapped Ernie. "It's too dark. There's not even a moon tonight."

"Technically, there is a moon," said Wilmer calmly. "It's just not visible since we've begun a new lunar phase. Did you know there is no such thing as a permanent 'dark side of the moon'? We can't see the far side of the moon, but it still gets sunlight. And a moon day lasts thirty days."

"You know so much," cooed Harriet. "But you mean each lunar day is twenty-nine-point-five earth days long, right?"

"Um, right. Sure," said Wilmer with a cough. "I was just rounding up a little."

"This is really fascinating stuff," said Vlad with

an exaggerated yawn. "But can we head back? I hear
there are cider and doughnuts in the dining hall."

"Doughnuts?" said Ernie, snapping to attention. He took a few steps forward. "This way!"

"How do you know the way back?" asked
Wilmer.

Ernie shrugged.

"We need to figure this out scientifically," said
Wilmer sternly. He sank his hands into his pockets,
which felt like a good thinking pose, and was surprised to feel something small. Something wrapped.

It was a small chewy brown piece of candy.
"Want this?" Wilmer asked Ernie. "It's a homemade caramel."

Ernie shuddered. "From your mom? It's probably made from bologna. No way!"

Wilmer shrugged and put the candy in his own
mouth. "No, it's just a plain caramel. Not bad."

Ernie groaned.

"Can we get going?" asked Vlad with a snarl.
"Claudius and I need to get back to our exhibit."

"Oh, yes, we're *bursting* to get back." Claudius
chuckled.

Wilmer gave him an evil eye, but since it was so dark, Claudius couldn't see him, which sort of defeated the purpose. Wilmer scratched his chin. He regretted skipping the Science Night Hike seminar, but he'd solve their problem scientifically.

He wasn't the Amazing Wilmer Dooley for nothing.

Wilmer thought. He had read articles about being lost in the woods. What did they say? Moss grows on trees, right? The north side of trees. He bent down to look at the tree bark nearest him. He rubbed his hands against the trunk. "I feel moss here." He pointed in the direction of a tall radio tower that loomed high above the trees. "So we go in that same direction. That way is north."

"That's not really true," said Harriet. "Moss can grow anywhere. It generally prefers damp spots, and because of the position of the sun, the north sides of trees tend to be damper, but it's hard to always predict where moss will thrive."

Roxie pointed to the sky where a few stars were visible through the canopy of leaves overhead. "During the night hike seminar they said to look at the stars. That's the North Star. It's easy to find. You locate the Big Dipper. Which is there." She pointed up, and then drew an imaginary line through the heavens. "Connect the dots from the bottom to the top and follow that line to there. Which means we go this way." She pointed in the opposite direction Wilmer had pointed.

Wilmer jutted out his chin. "I think I know which way we should go," he barked, his brain clouding with anger. He took a few steps to his right.

"No, it's *this* way," snapped Roxie, taking a few steps in the opposite direction.

"You're not even a scientist! Who would listen to you?" Disdain dripped from Wilmer's tongue. "C'mon, everyone. Let's go!" He took a few more steps. "Who's going with me?"

No one answered. No one followed.

"I'm going with Roxie," said Vlad.

Roxie's voice bounced through the air like a fragrant flower. "I knew *you* would. It's nice to have someone believe in you." She said this with so much meaning, it felt like a stick had jabbed Wilmer in the heart.

CHAPTER FOURTEEN

Science Night Hike Basics
By Elvira Padgett

Although this is the first year the science fair is at the Sac à Puces Palladium, Lodge, and Resortlike Hotel, the Science Night Hike is a consortium tradition. I only wish I could hike with all of you, but I'm way too busy planning things, and I'm no scientist! I know you will all love it. In forty-five years only one student has been lost! (And little Teddy Thornberry was found three years later living cheerfully with a family of coyotes, so he barely counts.)

We don't have any coyotes around here— just bears and poisonous snakes, and only a few of each. But follow these simple rules and getting back will be easy!

- Bears usually avoid humans unless they are looking for food, so don't smear mustard and relish all over your clothes and dress like a hot dog!

- Look to the stars. Follow the North
  Star and you'll soon find your way
  back.
- I love kids!
- Don't lose your chaperones. They have
  all been specially trained in first
  aid, navigation, and safety.
- Listen carefully for announcements
  from our new PA system.
- I love kids!
  (I just had to write it again!)

Claudius smirked. Wilmer was making a fool of himself. Again. Insisting *his* direction was the right way back to the hotel. Maybe it was. Claudius had no idea. Moss this way. Stars that way. Who could keep track? He had barely paid attention during the Science Night Hike seminar. But he wouldn't follow Wilmer. Claudius wouldn't give his enemy the satisfaction! Some things were more important than cider and doughnuts.

But maybe he *should* follow Wilmer, for other reasons. Anything could happen: a bump on the head, Wilmer accidentally being tied up with rope and hung upside down from a tree branch, or put in a box and mailed to Brazil. Not that Claudius had rope or a box or stamps to pay for shipping. He smiled to himself at the thought of such deeds anyway.

He didn't wear an EVIL GENIUS shirt for nothing.

But Claudius didn't need any of that. He'd put Wilmer in his place tomorrow during the science fair, when his and Vlad's project would leave Wilmer in the dust. Or in the slime, to be exact. He grinned to himself again. Grinning to himself was one of his favorite things to do.

Vlad stood next to him. His cousin might be annoying at times—what was with those bow ties he wore?—but he *was* a good scientist. Claudius would give him that. He might even be a better scientist than Claudius, technically speaking.

But Claudius knew scientific knowledge was only a small part of scientific talent. The ability to connive and cheat and hoodwink the public . . . those were far more important attributes, and Claudius had them all.

No one could cheat and connive better than Claudius.

Claudius had told everyone he had cured the Mumpley epidemic, that Wilmer was full of himself and that he loved to pick his nose and kept a snot collection in jars. That last one was totally untrue, but when Claudius began making up stories about Wilmer, he found it difficult to stop. He told one boy that Wilmer had a vicious pet vampire bat, and another that Wilmer wasn't a kid but was actually a short adult named Raul who was wanted in fourteen states.

Claudius had been concerned that the other students might not believe his tall tales. They were a bit far-fetched—it was quite obvious that Wilmer didn't actually have robotic arms that shot laser beams—but Claudius was pretty convincing, and Wilmer had helped by acting all high and mighty. Kids were eager to believe the worst, and Claudius gave them exactly what they wanted. And then, when Wilmer knocked over Claudius's crystal experiment? Well, that had been the icing on the poisoned cake! Never mind that Claudius had somehow ruined his experiment way before Wilmer knocked it over, having made some pinkish-green muck that was not crystal-like in any way.

It was also surprising how quick to anger the other kids were. Scientists weren't normally violent. But these kids seemed ready to practically explode in hate.

Explode! Claudius chuckled to himself as he thought again of his science exhibit.

He would be crowned the science fair champion, as Wilmer looked on jealously. Claudius would show his father he could be a success! Why, Dr. Dill would be so busy congratulating Claudius, he might even forget to answer his phone for the first time ever.

Claudius saw a large radio tower soaring up into the sky. It seemed a bit out of place in the middle of a forest. It was enormous. Claudius shivered. He was afraid of heights.

"We're all going *this* way," said Claudius, walking in the direction Roxie suggested.

"What about you, Ernie?" demanded Wilmer.

Ernie looked at Wilmer and then at Roxie. He hesitated. "I think Roxie is right. And I really want doughnuts."

"Fine. I don't want you to come anyway," Wilmer snapped. "When you get lost, don't go yelling to me for help! How about you, Harriet? Are you going with them too?"

Harriet stepped toward Wilmer. "Of course not. You *are* the Amazing Wilmer Dooley, after all."

"Yes, I am," agreed Wilmer.

Ernie and Roxie groaned. Claudius smirked.

"But, Wilmy. I think you might be mistaken," Harriet continued. She quickly added, "Just this once." She pointed to the tree bark next to her. "This moss is growing in a different direction than the moss on the first tree. And at the seminar they said—"

"I should have known!" yelled Wilmer. "You're just like them!" He pointed to Claudius and Vlad. "Working against me. All of you are."

"You're acting like a baby!" yelled Ernie.

"Just forget it!" Wilmer shouted. "Forget all of it and all of you. I'm going my way. And if you all get eaten by bears, it's not my problem!"

And Wilmer stomped off into the woods. Alone.

CHAPTER FIFTEEN

WARNING!

NEVER WALK IN THESE WOODS ALONE.
ALWAYS GO WITH A PARTNER, PREFERABLY
ONE WHO IS A TRAINED BEAR WRESTLER,
OR BETTER YET, WITH GROUPS OF FIVE OR
MORE TRAINED BEAR WRESTLERS. THESE
WOODS ARE TEEMING WITH:

BEARS

SNAKES

POISON IVY

HIDDEN TREE ROOTS AND THINGS
YOU CAN TRIP ON

A LARGE RADIO TOWER
(NO TOUCHING, PLEASE!)

BIG, HAIRY SPIDERS

THINGS THAT GO BUMP IN THE NIGHT

A PARTICULARLY CRABBY SKUNK
NAMED IVAN

Wilmer regretted his behavior immediately. He had acted like a jerk.

To make matters worse, he was now by himself in a scary forest, without a flashlight, and was completely lost.

Why had Wilmer been so stubborn, anyway? Why couldn't he clear the clouds of irritation that hovered in his brain?

And not just any clouds—threatening cumulonimbus clouds.

It's Claudius's fault. Everything is Claudius's fault! He'll be sorry he messed with me!

Wilmer concentrated on removing the anger from his brain. He walked forward. It was hard to see in this blackness, and he nearly stumbled over a tree root. Wait. He had passed this tree root earlier. Which meant that just a few steps away was that tall radio tower. It must be nearly a thousand feet high. Yes, there it was. He was going in circles.

He knelt down and rubbed his hand against some tree bark, feeling the fuzzy moss that covered it. Harriet was right. This moss was not on the same side as the other moss.

Why had he skipped that Science Night Hike seminar?

Roxie had suggested looking at the stars. Wilmer wasn't an astronomer—his specialty was chemistry. But she said to find the Little Dipper and go down . . . or was it the Big Dipper and go up? Or was it Orion's belt and go left? Or was it the second star to the right and straight on till morning?

It didn't matter. He was inside such a thick clump of trees he couldn't even see the sky. He continued walking.

Moaning.

Wilmer heard it from behind a tree nearby.

Was it a bear? It didn't sound like a bear, but what did a bear sound like, anyway?

Should he run, or confront the beast? Dogs sensed fear. Did bears? Maybe Wilmer should take control and charge the bear. He did the math in his head. If it were a bear and he ran, there was a 75 percent chance of being hunted down, but if he confronted the bear, there was a 45 percent chance the bear would run off. Those were just random numbers, but they made Wilmer feel better about his course of action. He shuffled toward the tree, his heart racing.

There. The animal was on the ground, sitting next to a tree. Maybe it had fallen on the same tree root that had almost tripped Wilmer. He should run. He could make it. He was about to spin around when he heard a wheeze.

"Ernie!" cried Wilmer. His best friend held his ankle. "What are you doing here?"

"Injuring myself," said Ernie with a groan. "I tripped over this tree root."

"But why are you here?"

"To find you, what do you think? You were going the wrong way."

"But I was a jerk," said Wilmer.

"I said mean things too. I've felt grouchy all day. But the fresh air seems to be helping." He paused and then shouted, "You stink!"

"What?" said Wilmer, recoiling.

"Nothing," said Ernie, seemingly oblivious to the words that had just blared from his mouth.

Wilmer looked at this friend, worried. They needed to get back. "Can you get up?"

"I don't think so," groaned Ernie. "My ankle is killing me. You should go ahead. Save yourself."

"Save myself?"

"That's what they always say in the movies. One guy breaks his leg and tells the other guy to save himself."

"Well, you didn't break your leg, and the only thing we're in danger of is missing doughnuts."

Ernie shivered. "A fate worse than death."

"We should make a splint."

Wilmer searched the ground. Despite the inky dark, he quickly found a small but sturdy stick. Then he removed one of his socks and used it to tie the stick to Ernie's ankle. As he worked, he forgot about this crankiness. It was just him and Ernie now, doctor and patient. Wilmer was born to be a doctor.

"That'll keep your ankle steady," said Wilmer, helping Ernie to his feet. "How does it feel?"

Ernie took a step forward. He winced as he put pressure on his ankle. "Not the most comfortable way to walk," he admitted. "But better." Suddenly, he frowned and yelled, "Must spoil milk!"

"What?" asked Wilmer, alarmed.

"Nothing," said Ernie. He smiled, appearing to have no memory of his disturbing shout, and then held out his thumb.

Wilmer gave it a vigorous shake back. It felt good to be best friends with Ernie again, but he still needed to find out what was happening.

"Lean against me as we walk," Wilmer said.

Ernie put his arm around Wilmer's shoulders and they took a step forward. Wilmer looked at the tall trees and charcoal dimness around them. "Um. You don't happen to know the way back, do you?" asked Wilmer.

"I was hoping *you* did," said Ernie with a frown. "I'm completely lost."

"Me too," moaned Wilmer. "I guess I don't know *everything.*"

"Even the smartest person in the world doesn't know *everything.* There are just too many things to know."

Wilmer sighed. He knew even the greatest scientists weren't right 100 percent of the time. Albert Einstein once insisted the universe wasn't expanding, but most scientists think it is. Einstein called it his "biggest blunder." If Albert Einstein hadn't known stuff, then it was okay that Wilmer didn't know stuff, too.

Scientists observed. Wilmer just needed to observe and he'd find his way back.

He hadn't been doing very much observing lately.

Wilmer plunged his hand into his back pocket. That's where he often kept his small magnifying glass, although he had left it at home. Instead, he found a wrapped strawberry-colored hard candy. A small bit of string tied a note around it. Wilmer squinted to read in the dark: Don't have a hard time this weekend. Love, Mom.

Ernie grabbed the treat. "I'm not missing out on candy again," he said, tearing open the plastic and popping the candy in his mouth. Within seconds he coughed, gagged, and spit it out. "Help! Help!"

"Mom's fish-oil-and-strawberry-shoe-polish hard bites," said Wilmer with a nod. "Not one of my favorites."

Ernie's violent coughs were drowned out by a

deafening loudspeaker crackle from the enormous radio tower nearby. Wilmer was glad he'd brought his earplugs; he quickly plunged them inside his ears.

"Cover your ears!" he yelled to Ernie, but it was too late: Ernie was already staring blankly forward, drool dripping onto his collar.

Despite his earplugs, the sound was so loud that Wilmer's ears quivered. His brain turned fuzzy. His vision grew cloudy. He wanted to punch someone. He staggered forward, as if his entire soul had been wrenched out of his body, barfed onto a nearby tree, and then pecked by woodpeckers.

It was not a good feeling.

"Attention, dear, dear students," spoke the voice, as garbled and distorted as ever. "Doughnuts and cider are being served. Also, eat apples every day for healthy teeth, and make fruit baskets for people with sinus congestion."

"Fruit has plenty of antioxidants to help combat colds," said Wilmer.

The voice stopped, the final squeal faded away, and Wilmer felt his wits return. "Man, what was that?" he asked, wiping sweat from his brow. "That jarred my head even more than usual. Do you think it's because we're so close to this tower, Ernie? Ernie?"

Ernie stared forward, his eyes bulging. He reminded Wilmer of a zombie, but with less color.

Wilmer looked at Ernie uneasily and poked him on the shoulder. Ernie hissed.

"Ernie! Buddy!" yelled Wilmer. "Snap out of it!"

But Ernie didn't snap out of anything. He kept staring forward with glassy, emotionless eyes. "Must smash pumpkins," he mumbled. "Must belt buckles."

"Ernie?" gasped Wilmer. "What are you talking about?"

Ernie glared and cracked his knuckles. "Must batter pancakes."

There was menace in his voice, a low rasp that made Wilmer uneasy. They needed to get back, and fast. Wilmer grabbed Ernie's hand. "Come on!" Ernie stumbled forward.

But which way was back? Wilmer still had absolutely no idea.

CHAPTER SIXTEEN

DANGER!
BEYOND THIS POINT: RADIO FREQUENCY
FIELDS MAY EXCEED ALL POSSIBLE SAFETY
RULES FOR HUMAN EXPOSURE. IN FACT,
WE CAN PRETTY MUCH GUARANTEE
THAT THEY DO.

ALSO WATCH OUT FOR: LOOSELY BURIED
ELECTRICAL WIRES AND CABLES,
RADIOACTIVE CONTAMINATION, FALLING
BOLTS, LOOSE SCREWS, LOUD NOISES,
AND PIGEON DROPPINGS.

FAILURE TO OBEY THIS SIGN MAY RESULT
IN SERIOUS INJURY AND OTHER
UNPLEASANTRIES. SO STAY AWAY
FROM THIS TOWER IF YOU KNOW
WHAT'S GOOD FOR YOU.

Wilmer approached the radio tower. It was massive
and imposing, like a giant iron monster camouflaged

in the darkness. Ernie trudged next to him. Although it was just a steel structure, something about it raised the hairs on the back of Wilmer's neck. He placed his fingers against the metal, the steel icy to the touch.

"Cracks," mused Wilmer, feeling thin slivers spreading throughout the base. "That's odd. I guess this radio tower must be as old as the hotel. Maybe older." He closed his eyes and concentrated. It felt good to exercise his science brain muscles. It would have felt even better if Ernie wasn't staring at him and mumbling strange, slightly frightening things.

"Must waste baskets."

Oddly, Ernie kept Wilmer calm. He felt his own anger bubbling inside him, but Ernie's craziness was a reminder that he needed to keep those emotions under control. As a scientist, he had spent his entire life making unemotional, science-based decisions, and he needed to keep it that way. He was a trained scientist, after all! Ernie was depending on him. And maybe everyone else was too.

Wilmer spoke out loud to himself. The sound of his voice made the evening feel less frightening.

"Observation. That's the key to scientific discovery," he muttered. "Like Columbus discovering the new world by crashing into it. Of course, that was a bit hard to miss, what with it being a giant continent in the middle of the ocean. You'd really have to be a lousy observer to miss that one."

"Must crush velvet," murmured Ernie with an eerie, threatening-sounding purr.

Wilmer barely heard his friend. The gears in his head spun rapidly. "So, what can we observe here? There's an old radio tower in the middle of the forest. But we don't get any reception for electronics. You'd think a tower of this size would produce radio waves that could reach miles away. So maybe . . ." Wilmer's brain neurons were firing quickly. It felt good to be lost in scientific thinking. "Maybe this doesn't use radio signals at all. Maybe it's a closed system used only to amplify announcements from the hotel, so that they can be heard for miles. In that case this tower would use telephone lines or cables—"

"Must crash helmets," mumbled Ernie.

"Will you be quiet?" grumbled Wilmer. He

needed some light. If only Ernie had a flashlight.

"Must engulf Mexico." Ernie moaned.

But Ernie had something that would work just as well as a flashlight.

"Ignore me," Wilmer mumbled as he plunged his hand into Ernie's jacket pocket. Ernie snarled, but didn't stop Wilmer's searching arm. Finally, Wilmer pulled out a crumbling, glowing-orange Marmalade ChocoBUZZZZ! cupcake.

Its light was even brighter than a flashlight.

Basked in the glow of the chocolate dessert, Wilmer knelt down next to the tower. He was looking for wires, and after a few moments he found an assortment of colorful ones leading down the side of the tower and into the ground.

Ernie grunted. "Must box car kids."

"These cables must have been buried for decades," said Wilmer, so he was surprised when they lifted easily from under the soil, as if they had only recently been laid. "We're in luck. These should lead us back to the hotel. And if we hurry, maybe we can be back in time for doughnuts. Ready, Ernie?"

"Must jam traffic," muttered Ernie.

If the lure of doughnuts didn't wake up Ernie, then he *was* in bad shape.

Wilmer continued tugging on the wires, yanking them out of the dirt and following their trail through the forest. They weaved through the trees, around bushes, and over plants. Ernie plodded slowly behind. Soon the forest grew less dense, and the evening stars once again flickered overhead. *There* was the North Star, or at least what Wilmer thought was maybe the North Star. And shortly after that, the lights from the hotel glimmered in the nighttime air.

"We did it!" yelled Wilmer. "We're back!"

"Must butcher blocks," Ernie growled.

"You're really giving me the creeps," said Wilmer.

They crossed the wide-open lawn, Ernie trudging slowly and Wilmer stopping repeatedly to let him catch up. Finally, Wilmer pushed through the hotel doors. He hoped the smell of doughnuts wafting across the lobby might jar Ernie from his trance, but it had no effect. Meanwhile, Wilmer could see that the dining room was filled with kids.

Apparently, Wilmer and Ernie were the last to return. But the room was also surprisingly quiet. Dazed kids ate listlessly.

"Must burst bubbles," murmured Ernie.

Wilmer spied Vlad approaching and dove behind a giant plastic plant, pulling Ernie with him. Ernie had grabbed a seat cushion and was chewing on it quite happily, so he didn't object to being moved.

Wilmer peeked out from under a fake leaf. Vlad had exited the dining room, adjusted his bow tie, looked right and then left, and quickly dashed down the hall. Where was he going? He was acting very suspiciously, like always. And as scientists say, where there's smoke, there's fire.

Well, maybe scientists don't say that, but lots of people say that, many of whom are just as smart as scientists.

"We should follow him," said Wilmer to Ernie.

"Must steal curtains," said Ernie between cushion bites.

Wilmer shook his head. "Vlad went this way." Wilmer stepped out from behind the plant and hurried down the hall, stopped to wait for Ernie, then hurried again, and then stopped, hurried, stopped, and so on, until finally, after moving about ten feet, he said, "Hurry up. He'll get away."

"Must hurt lockers," muttered Ernie, seat cushion crumbling from his mouth. Wilmer sighed.

They continued to advance. Where was Vlad? The halls were lined with doors to various hotel rooms. He could be in any of them. There. One door was slightly ajar, with light streaming from the open crack. Wilmer almost missed it. It wasn't marked with a room number or a sign. It was probably a closet. Wilmer cautiously nudged the door open a few inches.

"Hello?" whispered Wilmer. "Anyone here?"

A soft beeping escaped from inside, but no voices, so Wilmer pushed the door open all the way and entered.

He gasped.

This wasn't a closet, but a state-of-the-art radio control room. This must be where all the loudspeaker announcements originated. A table in the middle of the room was covered with charts, graphs, and assorted papers. Against the far wall was a large radio control panel with a few hundred lights, buttons, and faintly blipping monitors displaying moving zigzag lines that resembled a heart monitor.

But that was only a small part of why Wilmer gasped.

Covering nearly an entire wall was a map of the world. Pins were placed all about, with different colored strings tied between them, crisscrossing the globe—a purple string led from New York to Hong Kong, an orange string from Phoenix to Bangladesh. Taped to the map was a note that read:

Today the hotel. Tomorrow the world! Mwa-ha-ha!

People laugh "Mwa-ha-ha," but they didn't usually take the time to write it down. That made the note much more disturbing.

There was also a map of the hotel grounds with complex mathematical notations written on the side that Wilmer didn't understand. A big, fat circle was drawn around the radio tower, with a big skull and crossbones over it and a note:

The final brain purge.

"That doesn't sound good," mumbled Wilmer.

Ernie staggered into the room behind him. He had finished eating his seat cushion and giant balls of foam covered his lips, creating a sort of foam mustache.

Wilmer closed the door behind them. He peered closely at a pie graph taped to a closet door that read:

Mind control: 94%
Minds turned to mush: 6%
Not bad!

In the corner were the initials *CD*.

"CD! Claudius Dill!" shouted Wilmer. Finally! Here was the proof he needed!

Wilmer heard footsteps clomping outside the door and out-of-tune whistling that sounded like an untalented ruby-throated hummingbird.

Scientific name: *Archilochus colubris.*

"That must be Vlad!" Wilmer exclaimed to Ernie. "We'll fight him! Together!" Wilmer flexed his arm, but failed to see a muscle.

Ernie drooled some more. "Must push daisies."

"Okay, never mind about the fighting. Quick! Hide!"

Ernie stared forward. "Must munch—"

"Yeah, yeah, whatever," Wilmer interrupted. He pushed Ernie toward the closet. The whistling outside the room grew louder and the doorknob clicked. The door swung open just as Wilmer closed the closet door in front of them.

CHAPTER SEVENTEEN

RESULTS OF MIND-CONTROL
WAVES ON MICE

Mouse 1 Deceased

Mouse 2 Deceased

Mouse 3 Deceased

Mouse 4 Deceased

Mouse 5 Deceased

Mouse 6 Deceased

Mouse 7 Deceased

Mouse 8 Deceased

Mouse 9 Deceased

Mice 10–768 Deceased

Mouse 769 ~~Alive!~~ Deceased

Mouse 770 Deceased

Mouse 771 Deceased

Mouse 772–902 Deceased

Mouse 903 ~~Alive! Alive! Alive!~~ Dead
as a doornail

Mouse 904 Deceased

Mouse 905 Deceased

Mouse 906 Deceased

Mouse 907 Deceased

Mouse 908 Deceased

Wilmer saw nothing but blackness in the cramped closet. Although Ernie was quiet, Wilmer didn't feel entirely safe hiding next to someone who had just eaten an entire seat cushion. Who knew what or *whom* Ernie might nibble on next?

But more importantly, what was Vlad doing?

Wilmer heard drawers opening, papers rustling, more whistling, a fart, and then the main door opening and closing again . . . and silence. After a few additional seconds of anxious waiting, Wilmer pushed open the closet door. He and Ernie fell out and onto the floor.

"Must pound cake," said Ernie. Wilmer tried to ignore his fuzzy-brained friend as he rose to his feet.

"Let's look around," suggested Wilmer.

He scanned the dozens of papers scattered about the table in the middle of the room. Random, half-finished mathematical formulas were scribbled on many of them. Wilmer was beginning to panic; he was a scientist, not a mathematician!

Wilmer picked up a report with the heading,

"Results of Mind-Control Waves on Mice." It listed 1,285 mice, with the word "Deceased" scrawled next to each.

He also found a few recipes for chicken soup.

But what did it all mean? Wilmer was sure there was something he was missing.

What had he heard when he hid in the closet? A fart. Whistling. A drawer opening.

A drawer!

There was a drawer on the side of the table, and Wilmer pulled the handle. It only opened a few inches. Wilmer yanked harder, but it was stuck.

Still, something was inside. Wilmer reached his hand into the drawer. He felt a notebook and slid it out.

His heart skipped three beats, beat twice, and then skipped once more. It wasn't just a notebook, but a scientific journal! Wilmer stared at it, his heart racing.

Scientific Journal Detailing My Evil Plan
CD

This was it! Claudius's own pen would spell out his evil plot!

With trembling hands, Wilmer opened the book. In messy, sprawling writing, it said:

Journal Log:
Our scheme is almost complete. After months of failure, we finally found the right loudspeaker frequency. The mice now do exactly what we say. Eat cheese! Run through a maze! Build a jet-powered mouse car!

Okay, they couldn't do the last one. But it wasn't from a lack of trying.

Mwa-ha-ha!

They must be brainwashed slowly. That's the key. We can't just hit them with the full frequency all at once. It's too strong! But with repeated low-level squeals and our commands, the mice become our slaves!

Permanently! Or their brains turn into soup. One or the other.

Actually, all the brains turn to soup eventually. But it takes longer this way.

The world has been filled with would-be villains. Genghis Khan! Attila the Hun! They had cunning and power and evil! But none of them had a brain-controlling loudspeaker soup-brain machine, like me. So I'm better than they are. Nyah-nyah-nyah!

No one suspects us, either.

But soon everyone will fear the name of—

There was a page missing from the book. It had been ripped right out! The entry concluded on the very last page of the journal:

We'll gather the smartest seventh graders in the entire state *to put our plan in motion. With all those sniveling little geniuses in our power, there won't be anyone left to stop us, except the stupider seventh graders.*

I would slap myself on the back with congratulations if my arms were longer. But they don't quite reach.

It's about time people bowed to me and acknowledged my greatness. Our greatnesses. The two of us! Together we shall rule!

CD

"Must squash rackets," purred Ernie.

"Not now, Ernie," snapped Wilmer. "Can't you see I'm busy?"

Wilmer stared at the journal. This was the proof he needed. Claudius had brainwashed mice! He had turned their brains into soup! He wasn't sure what all of it meant, other than something bad.

Wilmer needed to examine the room more thoroughly for details. But who knew when Vlad might return? Ernie wasn't looking well, either. "Just another minute," Wilmer promised his muddle-brained buddy.

"Must grate Gatsby," hissed Ernie.

Wilmer walked to the audio control panel and ran his hands gently over the dials. He didn't really understand how any of it worked and was hesitant to randomly press buttons. But the scientist who was afraid of making a mistake wasn't a very good scientist. Why, it took Thomas Edison over ten thousand failed attempts until he created his first lightbulb. Trial and error! That was one of the keys to scientific knowledge.

Of course, the error part was a problem, and why trials often led to exploding test tubes, scorched eyebrows, and feverish lab rats. Not all error ended well.

Oh, if only it was called "trial and succeed."

A giant red button attracted Wilmer's attention. It was the biggest on the console, more than twice the size of the others. "Here goes nothing," Wilmer said, pressing it.

A loud squeal erupted from the soundboard and Wilmer's head spun. He saw stars and felt woozy. His brain seemed lighter, as if it was escaping from his ears into a misty vapor. He staggered back, and as he did his finger lifted from the button. The sound stopped. Wilmer's head cleared.

"Did you feel that, Ernie?" asked Wilmer, dazed. "That must have been nearly the full-level frequency. But at least our brains aren't soup. I think." Wilmer rocked his head back and forth. "See? No splashing."

Two hands curled around Wilmer's neck.

"Must pulp fiction," grumbled Ernie, his fingers stiffening as they slowly closed around Wilmer's windpipe.

"Can't breathe . . . ," rasped Wilmer. "Don't . . . ," he croaked, trying to suck in air. He staggered back. Ernie bared his teeth. His fingers tightened. Wilmer pushed his hands back to keep himself from falling, and his palm accidentally grazed the big red console button again. "Ernie, stop!" he screamed as another loud squawk blared through the room.

Then, just as suddenly as his attack began, Ernie released Wilmer and stood like a statue.

Wilmer coughed and rubbed his raw neck. Ernie no longer seemed violent. He didn't seem much of anything, actually.

"Ernie?" probed Wilmer, waving his hand in front of his friend's face. "Are you going to try to kill me again?" Apparently he wasn't.

Wilmer needed to get back to his investigation. There were secrets to be solved! Brain puzzles to put together! But he needed to get Ernie back up to their hotel room before he went crazy again. Ernie was his best friend. They had exchanged thumb-shakes. Ernie had gone deep into the woods to find him. Sure, Ernie wasn't acting like himself, but it wasn't his fault. Ernie needed Wilmer, and Ernie needed to come first.

"We're going upstairs," said Wilmer.

"Must lame ducks," murmured Ernie, but he followed Wilmer obediently. "I'll be back," Wilmer said to himself, looking one last time at the room. "I'll solve this mystery. I must!" Then he growled, "Must whack moles."

He gasped. Why had he said *that*? He closed the door behind them and led Ernie down the hall, struggling to hold down the anger that wanted to burst out.

CHAPTER EIGHTEEN

Brain soup recipe
By CD
Serves 4

Ingredients:
Brain broth
1/4 tsp salt
1 leek
2 carrots
2 celery ribs
4 oz. noodles

Emit repeated high-dose frequencies, and put jar near ear to catch brain broth drippings. Add broth to soup pan, along with salt, leek, celery, and carrots. Bring to a boil and simmer for three hours. Add cooked noodles before serving.

In the lobby, kids milled about aimlessly. A flat-faced girl thumped into a wall over and over while yapping like an angry dog. Another kid—a short, stocky boy with a buzz cut—kept batting his own head with a sneaker. Two blond girls ate carpet fuzz.

Wilmer spied Roxie and Harriet. Neither seemed dazed or crazed. Good. Roxie must have worn her headphones during the last few announcements, and Harriet had her earplugs, which meant they had been protected from the evil loudspeaker squawks. Wilmer hurried over to them, waving his arms. "Hey! I need your help! Claudius and Vlad are planning on doing something bad with brain soup and mouse control and I'm not sure what else!"

Harriet folded her arms and turned her back to Wilmer. "You're just going to yell at me again."

He had forgotten about his behavior in the woods; that seemed so long ago! He had been mean and full of himself. But that was the old Wilmer. Well, no, not the old Wilmer. It had been the temporary new and horrible Wilmer. Actually, Wilmer still felt mean and combustible, but he was controlling it better now. So maybe he wasn't yet the old Wilmer. He was part old, part new. He became so confused that he just stared forward for a moment until he regained his thoughts. "Sorry. I'm back. No. Please. I need you guys to help me. That wasn't me in the woods."

"It wasn't you? It was a fake Wilmer? I suppose Claudius and Vlad created a robot Wilmer?" scoffed Harriet. "I'm not listening to you anymore."

"But the loudspeakers are turning everybody into mindless drones! Can't you see that? Don't you feel a ball of anger inside you, ready to explode?"

"Sure," said Harriet. "But I'm angry at *you*!"

"It's the loudspeakers," insisted Wilmer.

"The loudspeakers yelled at me in the woods?" asked Harriet, her hands on her hips.

"Well, no. But it's their fault!"

"Yesterday, whoever makes those announcements also suggested we give air fresheners to people with smelly feet. Why would an evil person say that?"

"Okay, you got me there. That would be useful. But I'm telling the truth! Just look at Ernie!"

"Must cuff links," mumbled Ernie.

"I'm not sure what Claudius and Vlad are planning," said Wilmer. "Not exactly. But it's bad."

Harriet stood, arms crossed, frowning. "I thought it was the loudspeakers' fault. Now it's Claudius's fault? Really, Wilmy. I'm so disappointed in you." She popped in her earplugs.

"Roxie! You can help!" pleaded Wilmer, turning to his one true love. Surely she would listen. She had to.

"I can't help. I'm not a scientist, remember?" Roxie crossed her arms and turned her back on Wilmer.

Wilmer grimaced. Had he really said that, to Roxie of all people? "Look. I was wrong. But don't you see that everyone here is acting like a brainwashed zombie . . . ?"

Next to them, a girl in a sparkly tank top licked a coffee table.

But Roxie wasn't listening. "I don't know what you're talking about." She pointed across the lobby. "Oh, look. There's Vlad! *He* cares about what I think." And she made a beeline to him and Claudius.

Wilmer's eyes narrowed. His enemies stood across the lobby, smirking as usual. The two cousins weren't acting brain-dead. They weren't staring blankly. That was more proof that they were behind all this! Vlad said something and Roxie laughed. Wilmer steamed. He should go over there right now and expose Vlad and Claudius for the evil monsters they were!

"We need to stop them!" screamed Wilmer, but no one paid him any attention.

Wilmer glanced at the walls, with their deep crevices and peeling paint. The ceiling was slightly slanted, and the floors felt uneven, as if the entire hotel was threatening to fall apart. Wilmer felt as ignored and helpless as the fractured plaster.

"Must snap dragons," murmured Ernie.

"We need—" Wilmer began again, before halting his words. What was the use? "Come on, Ernie," he said, leading his friend past four kids in matching Stephen Hawking baseball hats, who were snarling at an end table.

"Must fire flies," growled Ernie.

CHAPTER NINETEEN

Dear Journal,

I've stayed in the room with Ernie all night. He's stopped drooling and is now peacefully playing with his iNoise. Hopefully there won't be any of those awful announcements for a while.

But I need to put an end to this. Tomorrow is the science fair. I bet that's when Claudius and Vlad will make their final move, whatever that is.

I'll need to be ready.

But what can I do—I'm in over my head! And who knows how long I'll still have a head, at least one that's not soupy. According to Claudius's journal, brains need to be controlled slowly, with low-level frequencies. Which means that every time there's an announcement, everybody's brains become more twisted.

Last night a hotel broadcast suggested we write

letters to homesick penguins. That is a good idea. But what does it have to do with brain soup?

All I know for sure is that every time I hear a screech, I feel my arms weaken. Even with my earplugs, the noises are clouding my head. I won't be able to hold out forever. No one will.

The situation is getting more urgent by the minute. But how can I stop it alone? Ernie isn't in any condition to help. And Roxie and Harriet won't talk to me.

I'll have to expose Vlad and Claudius in the morning. Just one glance at the hotel's cracking walls reminds me that I need to crack this case. If it's the last thing I ever do.

But hopefully it won't be.

Signing off,

Wilmer Dooley

The next morning at breakfast kids ate quietly, with only a few signs of zombielike menace. No one seemed to remember the terror from the night before. One stocky boy wearing a shirt that said

HERE'S LOOKING AT EUCLID kept asking if anyone knew why part of his sneaker was eaten. A girl wearing a pink lab coat wondered why her tongue had carpet burn. Ernie kept picking seat cushion foam from his teeth.

The kids were still on edge, though. They grumbled at one another. They yelled mean things. Lizzy hurled a muffin at Tizzy.

Ernie had recovered a little from the previous night, but he was far from being himself. He gnawed on his sprinkled glazed doughnut slowly, in very un-Ernie-like fashion.

"Don't you want to cram that whole thing in your mouth and make a giant mess with the crumbs, and then eat four slices of extra-greasy bacon?" asked Wilmer.

Ernie shrugged. "I'm not hungry."

Yes, things were looking grim. Ernie wiped his mouth after eating a small bite of carrot cake.

And Ernie didn't like carrots.

Elvira and Mr. Sneed, on the other hand, seemed quite happy. They smiled. Mr. Sneed whistled a jaunty tune. They high-fived each other. Didn't the two adults see what was going on? They were probably just too excited for the science fair competition to pay attention. Wilmer should march over there right now and tell them all about Claudius's evil plan.

But they probably wouldn't listen either. They would just dismiss it as competition anxiety. Today was the big day, after all.

And Wilmer had left the proof back in the radio room.

Wilmer wished he could finish setting up his science project. He had spent so many hours on it, and he really wanted to win a new microscope. But stopping Claudius and Vlad was far more important. Wilmer was the students' only hope. He needed to get back to that room.

The loudspeaker squeaked, but this time Wilmer was extra-ready. He had created a second pair of earplugs using a torn bit of pillowcase and some rubber bands. He shoved his own pair into his ears, and then the second pair into Ernie's just before the announcement began. He wished he could have made enough for every ear in the hotel, but he didn't have enough time, or pillowcases.

"Attention, dear, dear students. Please set up your science projects. Judging will begin in forty-five minutes," said the announcer in its odd, electronically distorted voice. "And build a tree fort for a monkey because monkeys love tree forts."

Wilmer scratched his head. Why were monkeys important? Or maybe they weren't. Did Claudius and Vlad love monkeys? It didn't make any sense.

As the sound cut off, Ernie yanked the pillow stuffing from his ears. "Why'd you do that?"

"Saving you from turning into a violent jellyfish," said Wilmer. "Like last night."

Ernie scratched his forehead. "I don't remember anything about last night. But I was wondering why a tree branch was tied to my foot."

"Sorry, I forgot to remove it. But let me recap. Claudius and Vlad have built an elaborate loudspeaker system that wipes away brains. I think they've rigged that tall radio tower in the woods to broadcast their messages. They're going to blow up the hotel. And other things, too. Any of *that* ring a bell?"

Ernie looked unconvinced. "How could they possibly have done all those things?"

"I don't know," admitted Wilmer. "That is a flaw in my theory." Wilmer knew scientific facts did not have unexplained flaws. They were always accurate, proven time and time again. Consistent. The law of gravity didn't mean some apples fell from trees and others floated by. The law of planetary motion didn't mean some planets orbited the sun, and others went leaping around as they pleased.

But it *had* to be the two conniving cousins! The papers in the audio room were covered with the initials CD! Claudius Dill! A rose by any other name is still a rose! Not that Claudius Dill was a rose. No, he was a stinkbird, scientific name: *Opisthocomus hoazin.*

The stinkbird, an awkward chicken-size bird found in South America, is best known for its horrid, manurelike smell.

Yes, that's exactly what Claudius was: a stinky pile of cow poop.

Not that name-calling would help Wilmer save

the day. Still, it made him feel a little better.

But he couldn't sit around thinking of stink-birds, even if he wanted to. Wilmer needed to stop the cousins, and he needed to get back into the control room. He would find more evidence. He would show everyone that CD was guilty!

That'll show everyone I'm amazing. And I'll do it all by myself!

Stop. No. Where was that coming from? Was it the loudspeakers creeping into his head and turning him into someone he hated again? Or was it just his stupid ego bubbling up? Whatever it was, he needed to stop thinking like that. He needed help. He needed someone who understood sound.

And he knew two experts on that very subject: Harriet, Grand Newtonian winner for her project on sound waves, and Roxie, radio morning-show star.

They were still angry with him. He couldn't blame them, not after the way he had been acting. He had told Harriet his very best joke that morning, and she hadn't even smiled.

"What did the apple say to Sir Isaac Newton?" Wilmer had asked. "I'm falling for your law of gravity!"

Well, okay. Maybe it wasn't his very best joke, but the day before she would have been rolling in the aisles with laughter instead of rolling her eyes.

There she was now, heading to the exhibit hall. Wilmer jumped out of his chair. "Harriet! Wait!"

Harriet snarled at him. "I'm not talking to you, remember?"

"Technically, you are talking to me if you're telling me you're not talking to me," Wilmer pointed out. "I was a jerk. I'm sorry. I wish I could take it back. But kids are getting angrier than a bee with hives. Or something like that. I need to stop them before it becomes permanent. No. *We* need to stop them! Together. I can't do it without you."

Harriet folded her arms and glared at Wilmer. Then she looked around. Next to her, a girl punched the wall. Another girl stabbed the sofa with a pencil. "I admit people aren't exactly acting like themselves, but pressure will do that to you, like Elvira said. We all want to win."

And with that, she marched into the exhibit hall.

"Harriet—" cried Wilmer as he scrambled after her.

But as he stepped into the large hall behind her, his mouth dropped open.

The exhibits in the room were completely destroyed.

CHAPTER TWENTY

EXHIBIT HALL SAFETY RULES:
No running
No jumping
No ball playing
No poisonous gases, toxins, or mists
No deadly fungi
No peeking at other people's exhibits
No destroying anyone's exhibits
No blowing up the room
No peanuts
(some of our scientists have allergies)

Shattered glass layered the ground like crumbled ice. All the overhead light fixtures had fallen onto the exhibits, which now lay in broken heaps. It was hard to tell what had once been a science project and what had once been a light fixture. A terrarium had exploded and a large snake slithered about. Sculptures and models had fractured, splintered, and fallen. Jars had burst. It was like a tornado had spent the night.

A tornado named Claudius and Vlad!

They were probably in the radio room that very moment, preparing to carry out their sick, wretched plan that didn't entirely make sense. Why destroy the exhibits if they're just going to erase everyone's brains, anyway?

But no, there they were, over at their table. Claudius and Vlad hadn't even opened their box yet. Their project was probably in perfect condition and they were waiting for just the right moment to unveil it. They'd win by default!

"Ruined! All ruined!" sobbed a red-cheeked girl in the corner.

"Why? Why? Why?" cried a short boy with big, bushy eyebrows.

Harriet's exhibit was in a thousand pieces, having caught the tail end of a fallen light fixture. Bacteria samples lay in bubbling pools on the floor, sizzling like acid.

But Wilmer's project was in even worse shape. His projector lay in pieces among shattered glass slides. His tall fiberglass displays had cracked.

His jar of leeches had shattered, and a swarm of them oozed among the broken equipment.

"Help!" cried Lizzy, standing behind Wilmer. "Get it off! Get it off!" A leech was on her arm.

"No worries," said Wilmer. "It's only sucking your blood. It'll fall right off after it has gorged itself."

She fainted.

Enough was enough! Wilmer needed to put a stop to this once and for all. He pointed to Claudius and Vlad. He raised his voice to a scream. "They did this! They've been plotting all weekend to blow up the hotel and brainwash everyone! Claudius and Vlad. The twin terrors! The diabolical duo! They must be stopped!"

A hush filled the room. All eyes locked on Wilmer, and then on Claudius and Vlad. They had to believe Wilmer now! It was the only way to stop the scheme that Wilmer was still confused about.

"But if they're brainwashing us, why would they destroy the exhibits?" asked a boy in the back of the room.

"Well, I haven't figured that out," admitted Wilmer.

"We haven't done a thing!" yelled Vlad.

"Oh yeah?" Wilmer's voice, which was already loud, grew even louder and angrier. He balled his hands into fists. His brain, which he had been trying to control all morning, bubbled with fury. But he didn't care anymore. He marched past his table to the cousins' exhibit, avoiding shards of glass, a pile of dissected frogs, six cracked eggs, a fractured model of the solar system, and other assorted rubble. "If you are innocent, then why are all of our exhibits destroyed, and not yours!" He grabbed the box that covered their project, hoisted it up, and slammed it to the ground.

A tall black clay mountain stood on their table in perfect condition. The kids in the room gasped. A cloud of anger rose like thick, ashy smoke. Wilmer sneered in glorious triumph. He pounded his fist on their table. Here was proof!

But the force of Wilmer's hand made the desk tremble. Its legs teetered. Claudius stepped forward with his hands outstretched, but it was too late. The legs snapped, the desk fell over, and the mountain toppled to the ground, smashing into a worthless heap of pebbles.

"Whoops," said Wilmer.

"Our volcano!" cried Vlad.

"It was going to spew lava all over the room!" groaned Claudius.

"It would have blown chunks of slime!" moaned Vlad.

"It would have exploded awesome ooziness!" wailed Claudius.

"It would have been gloriously yucky!" cried Vlad.

Wilmer was stunned. "B-b-but . . ."

The kids in the room glared at Wilmer. Snorts of rage blew from their nostrils. Spittle of wrath flew from their lips.

"Making groundless accusations is not science!" cried Lizzy, now awake and starting to stand up. She looked at her arm. "Eeeek! A leech!" She fainted again.

"Well, maybe I made a mistake," admitted Wilmer. "But they're still trying to control your brains!"

"It was Wilmer who did this!" declared Claudius. "He didn't eat doughnuts last night. Where was he? Sabotaging the exhibits?"

"I was lost outside," said Wilmer with a gulp, his voice catching in his throat.

But no one listened. A few kids pounded fists into palms, others picked up broken objects from the ground. Sometimes battles can be won. Other times it pays to know when to retreat. This was one of those times. Embarrassed, humiliated, and worried for his safety, Wilmer turned on his heels and sprinted out of the room.

CHAPTER TWENTY-ONE

PADGETT!
Join everyone's favorite biology expert,
Valveeta Padgett, for another fun-filled hour
of science and mah-jongg. On today's very
special episode of *Padgett!*, your favorite
science celeb will explain the madcap
world of frog legs, and how understanding
these hopping amphibian limbs can improve
your mah-jongg game by leaps and bounds.
*Check your local cable listings
for channel and time.*

Mrs. Valveeta Padgett smiled. This day was turning
out much better than she had ever imagined.

First, she reflected on the television script
notes she had written that morning. They were
good. In fact, this episode of *Padgett!* might just
be her best ever. Comparing mah-jongg to the mat-
ing habits of snails might not be the most obvious
subject for a hit television show, but in her brilliant hands it didn't only work, it was magnificent.

She'd probably win an Emmy. Maybe two.

But even more delightful than her extraordinary writing and those fascinating snails was the scene unfolding in front of her.

Earlier she had been aghast at the wreckage that filled the hall. The kids' agony was heartbreaking. But then Mrs. Padgett thought some more. Maybe things weren't that bad. It would be easier to judge a science fair if there were no fair to be held. She had enjoyed the free food, but she had dreaded the idea of mingling with children all day while looking at their exhibits. Now she could work on her television scripts, which was a much better use of her time.

But the best part was Wilmer Dooley. The fool! Making baseless accusations that spun around the room only to knock him back like a boomerang. Disgraced! Humiliated! She had noticed strange behavior from the kids earlier, so when Wilmer accused Claudius and Vlad of mischief, she hadn't blinked an eye. Sabotage? Some sort of brainwashing plan? She expected such industriousness from Claudius. There was a kid who was going places!

But Wilmer was completely wrong, which was even better. Oh, the joy! Mrs. Padgett especially admired Claudius's quick thinking, turning the tables on Wilmer by accusing *him* of this disaster. Sheer genius!

And Claudius was hardly a genius. Not normally, anyway.

Some snot-filled kid ran up to her, interrupting her reverie. He tugged his hair in distress. His eyes were red from crying. "What are we going to do, Mrs. Padgett? What happened?"

Mrs. Padgett bent down and spoke in a soft, soothing tone. "Well, it's hard to say. I would hate to think that Wilmer Dooley was behind this disaster, wouldn't you? Of course, I've heard rumors that Wilmer Dooley's recent celebrity has gone straight to his head. Some people simply can't handle fame. I can, of course, and I handle it quite nicely, thank you. I will be happy to give you an autograph later if you'd like, but now is not the time.

"Still, even if the boy is a menace—and I'm not saying he is, mind you, I'm just repeating what I've heard—I can't imagine Wilmer Dooley would be capable of such depravity, can you?" She waved her hand grandly. "Now, I would never spread rumors like this one: 'Wilmer Dooley is completely nuts and has single-handedly destroyed the fair.' No, not I!"

The snot-stuffed child pulled at his hair some more and then ran off to blabber to a group of kids. Mrs. Padgett hoped he wasn't spreading horrible, unfounded rumors about Wilmer ruining the science fair. And she hoped that group of kids wouldn't then prattle to other groups of kids and that soon, like a giant game of telephone, everyone would turn against Wilmer even more than they had already.

Oh, Mrs. Padgett would hate for that to happen. She snickered and smiled broadly.

Maybe Mrs. Padgett should agree to judge science fairs more often. She couldn't remember the last time she'd had such fun.

Wilmer sat on a half-eaten chair in the lobby. Shouts from the exhibit hall buzzed through the air like angry wasps.

Wilmer stomped his foot in frustration, and felt something rub against his toes. He removed

his shoe, surprised to find a small folded piece of
paper wedged inside. It was a handwritten note.

Dear Wilmer,
  I know you'll have a lot of fun
this weekend. We are so excited
that you were nominated for this
prestigious science fair.
  As you know, being a good
person is just as important as
being a good scientist. And you're
both! We are so proud. Just
remember, if you ever stumble
in life or in science; observe!
Observation can solve any puzzle.
  Never jump to conclusions unless
you have observed first—fairly,
objectively, and carefully. That's
the first and most important rule
of science, and of life.
  But you know that already.
Love,
Dad

A lump grew in Wilmer's throat, too big to
swallow. His dad was right, of course. Observation
could solve any problem. But then why was Wilmer
in such trouble? He *had* observed, hadn't he? He

had used scientific reasoning to conclude that Vlad and Claudius were guilty beyond all doubt.

If the sun set in the west one day, it would set in the west for the next million years! If Claudius was guilty of evilness once, he was guilty of all evil forever. Those were facts culled from observations.

Maybe. Probably. No, not really. Those weren't facts. They were predictions. Besides, the sun doesn't move at all. The earth does. So really, the sun doesn't set, since it's just up there minding its own business. More accurately, one could say the Earth spins counterclockwise, creating the appearance of a setting and rising sun, and would remain spinning should gravitational forces remain constant.

What proof did Wilmer have that Claudius and his cousin were the masterminds behind this entire plan, whatever it was? Some initials and a hunch. That was all.

But that was enough, wasn't it? Wilmer slapped his hand on his knee. Of course it was enough!

"Are you okay?" Harriet stood over Wilmer.

"You slapped your knee. It looked painful."

"Oh. Hi," said Wilmer. "My knee is okay, thanks. Have you come to laugh at me and make me feel worse than I already do? You might as well."

Harriet sat next to Wilmer. She took his hand in hers and rubbed it gently. "Wilmy. Darling. I'm sorry. I don't know why I've been so mad. Science is all about trial and error, right? Just because you've made a few errors doesn't mean I should turn my back on you. Did Edison give up after ten thousand attempts at building the lightbulb? Of course not. And on the ten thousand and first attempt, he nailed it. Or maybe the ten thousand and forty-seventh. Really, I'm not sure exactly. But you're onto something. Someone *is* trying to control our minds. Someone did destroy the exhibit hall. But are you sure it's Claudius and Vlad?"

"Of course I'm sure," insisted Wilmer. "I saw Vlad go down that hall the other night. That's how I found the radio control room. What else would Vlad be doing?"

Harriet shrugged. "I don't know. The boys' bathroom is over there too."

"But I found journals describing the plan with Claudius's initials. CD! Explain that!"

The loudspeaker erupted with its signature squeak. Wilmer stiffened. His brain flipped. He and Harriet shoved in their earplugs.

"Attention, dear, dear students," spoke the eerie voice. "Always wear seat belts, and whole wheat bread has more fiber."

The message ended as suddenly as it begun. Wilmer and Harriet popped out their earplugs and exchanged confused glances. "What does all that mean?" asked Wilmer.

"Well, it means you should eat wheat bread and not white bread if you need to add fiber to your diet," said Harriet. "And statistically speaking, seat belts reduce deaths and injuries by about fifty percent."

"No," said Wilmer. "I mean, why does Claudius, or Vlad, or . . . someone else, maybe . . . keep telling us these things? My dad always says 'observe.' And my observation tells me there's more to that cheerful advice than meets the eye. Or rather, than meets the ear."

"Oh! There you are!" Roxie, walking briskly across the lobby from the exhibit hall, waved to Wilmer and Harriet. "Ernie and I were worried about you, Wilmer. A lot of kids are mad. Ernie was setting them straight, though. He told them you would never destroy an exhibit hall, and that you guys were together all night."

"Really? Ernie's speaking up for me?" Wilmer's heart lifted a little.

"Well, he *was*," said Roxie. "But then he started acting all funny and saying 'Must mash potatoes.' Lizzy and Tizzy are snarling like wolves. Those guys with the matching Stephen Hawking baseball caps are just staring at the floor and drooling."

"It's the loudspeaker announcements," said Wilmer. "They're warping everyone's brains."

Roxie snapped her fingers. "I thought something was going on! That garbled loudspeaker voice! I figured it either meant someone was planning a horrible scheme or the loudspeakers were broken. I keep putting on my headphones to block out the noise. I get so mad when I think about it!"

Wilmer nodded. "That's the loudspeakers' fault. They're making everyone angry."

"Maybe I can help?"

Nothing would make Wilmer happier than working with Roxie. They would crack this conundrum together. Just like Romeo and Juliet! Cleopatra and Caesar! Except with science and brainwashing thrown in.

But Wilmer hadn't the nerve to tell any of that to Roxie. He looked sheepishly at his shoes. "Um, yes. Sure," he sputtered. "Science and journalism are both about observation. We would make a great team."

"*We?*" Suddenly, Harriet scowled. She hissed. She gnashed her teeth. She clenched her fist.

"Harriet?" gasped Wilmer. Had her brain fallen back under the loudspeaker's spell?

Harriet let out a deep breath. "Sorry. Not sure what happened there. I suppose you're both right. Roxie would be a great help. Three heads are better than two." She glared at Roxie again. "But Wilmy is mine, got it?" She grabbed Wilmer's hand and yanked him out of his chair. "Let's go to the radio control room, honey."

"Honey?" Wilmer gulped. Harriet snarled, and Wilmer decided it was better not to argue. "Sure, honey," he said meekly.

They hurried down the hallway.

"The room is this way," Wilmer told Roxie. "That's where Claudius and Vlad have been doing their dirty work."

"Claudius and Vlad?" asked Roxie in surprise. "When I asked Mr. Sneed if I could put on my *Mumpley Musings* radio show over the loudspeakers, he said no one was allowed near the audio controls except him."

"But I found Claudius's initials in the room!" insisted Wilmer. "CD!"

"Maybe that's for Clarence Dillard, as in Clarence Dillard Sneed," suggested Roxie.

Wilmer hit his palm on his forehead. "Argh!" he yelled. "Of course!"

"Are you okay?" asked Harriet. "That was some powerful forehead slapping. And you slapped your leg earlier. Are the loudspeakers making you do that?"

Wilmer shook his head. "No, that's just me being upset." To Roxie he said, "Did Mr. Sneed say anything else? Every detail is important. That's why observation is so crucial to scientific discovery."

Roxie tapped her finger to her chin, thinking. "He said something about the radio tower. Let me see. He said that after a final announcement from the tower, we would have soup. Yes, that's it. Something about seventh-grade soup. He cackled when he said it, which struck me as odd, but then I figured he just really liked soup and it was going to be the lunch special."

Wilmer gulped. Seventh-grader-brain soup.

They rushed farther down the hall, narrowly avoiding Lizzy, who was trying to eat a tape dispenser.

"Hurry!" yelled Wilmer. He pointed to the closed, unmarked door. He reached it, grabbed the doorknob, and twisted as hard as he could.

It didn't move. The door was locked.

CHAPTER TWENTY-TWO

The world has been filled with would-be villains. Genghis Khan! Attila the Hun! They had cunning and power and evil! But none of them had a brain-controlling loudspeaker soup-brain machine, like me. So I'm better than they are. Nyah-nyah-nyah!

No one suspects us, either.

But soon everyone will fear the name of—

Observation.

That's what scientists do when solving a puzzle, and unlocking a locked door was just a scientific puzzle. All Wilmer needed was observation.

And a key. That would be helpful.

But there wasn't even a keyhole. Wilmer stared at the smooth round knob. How could he get in? He slammed his fist against the door in anger.

Think! Wilmer needed to use his slightly clouded brain. What had he observed earlier when he was in the radio control room?

Well, nothing. He had thrown himself into a closet with Ernie.

But observation wasn't just about seeing things. It was about using all your senses. For instance, he had observed that Ernie needed to brush his teeth. Being in that cramped closet with Ernie's stale breath had been very unpleasant.

What else? Whistling. Wilmer had heard it coming from Vlad. No, not Vlad, but Mr. Sneed. Maybe the sound of whistling triggered some sort of automatic locking device?

Wilmer had read that a specific combination of musical sounds could open certain locks. He remembered that Mr. Sneed had whistled like a ruby-throated hummingbird. Wilmer whistled, although it was mostly air and gurgling. He wasn't much of a whistler.

"Thrwat, thrfft . . ."

"I enjoy a little music," said Roxie. "But maybe we should be breaking into the room and not breaking into song?"

Wilmer continued whistling, or rather trying to:

". . . Splsshhh whooot fllpptt . . ."

Nothing happened.

"No offense, but you're a horrible whistler," said Harriet. "Let me show you. It's all about cheek vibrations. You direct your airflow around your tongue, like so . . ."

She whistled. It sounded just like a common house sparrow, flitting about. Scientific name: *Passer domesticus.*

"And by a simple repositioning of the tongue tip, you can change the pitch, like so . . ." Harriet whistled again; this time it sounded like an eastern bluebird. Scientific name: *Sialia sialis.*

"Can you whistle like a ruby-throated hummingbird?" pleaded Wilmer.

"That's an odd request," said Harriet. "But for you, Wilmy dear, anything, even if it means whistling like an *Archilochus colubris.*"

Harriet whistled, and the soft purr of birdlike chirps melodically floated through the hall.

The door clicked and popped open.

"See?" said Harriet. "Whistling is easy, but when you position your tongue too closely to the front teeth, it prohibits the airflow that you need to—"

"Can we just go inside?" asked Roxie.

They stepped into the control room. The pile of papers on the center table looked fuller and messier than before, with many carelessly knocked on the floor. "Harriet and I will tackle the papers," said Wilmer. "Roxie, you try to figure out the control panel. You're the radio expert."

"But *I'm* the sound expert," protested Harriet with a haughty nose lift. "That's much more impressive, scientifically speaking." She thrust her finger toward Roxie. "And don't you forget it."

Wilmer sighed, but he and Harriet began searching through the scattered pages while Roxie examined the console.

"I can't make heads or tails of these," admitted Wilmer, looking through the charts and mathematical formulas that littered the tabletop.

"The graphs show sound waves," explained Harriet. "They represent various wavelengths and frequencies. And there are tiny notations on the side. See?" She held a page and squinted to read it. "This one says, 'Pitch sixteen turns brains into spaghetti.'"

"If they created a sound that turns brains into pasta, I guess they really used their noodle," said Wilmer with a laugh.

"Not now, Wilmy," said Harriet.

Wilmer held up other pages with graphs and notes. One said, *Pitch 428: turns brains into milk shakes.* Another said, *Pitch 142: turns brains into baklava.*

"All this looking is making me hungry," said Wilmer. "But we need to find the particular pitch that *controls* brains. It has to be here somewhere."

"Keep looking," said Harriet. "It's a remarkable discovery, and could be of immense scientific value."

"Except that it can also be used to turn brains into soup," said Wilmer.

"That is a drawback," agreed Harriet. "But it is still impressive."

"What does this do?" asked Roxie. She pointed to the bright red button in the middle of the console.

"Don't press that!" warned Wilmer, but it was too late. A loud squeal erupted and Wilmer's ears felt like shattering glass. His brain turned numb and he staggered back. So did Harriet. Roxie winced and turned another knob. The pitch went higher and Wilmer's brain felt like it was swimming in quicksand. Roxie nudged another knob and the pitch of the noise changed again. Wilmer felt pressure in his skull as if his brain was blowing up like a balloon. Roxie released her finger from the button, the noise ceased, and Wilmer's brain felt normal again.

"Sorry," said Roxie. "I wanted to see what would happen."

"Well, please don't do that again," Wilmer begged. "We shouldn't tamper with these frequencies. Who knows what they'll do?"

"I don't want spaghetti or soup brains," agreed

Harriett. "We need to keep looking!" They continued rifling through pages until Harriet pointed to the table drawer. "What's in here?" She tried to slide it open but it stopped after a few inches.

"It's stuck," explained Wilmer.

Harriet dug her hand inside the drawer and felt around. "There's something in the track. Hold on. . . ." She moved her hand around, tugging and grunting, and finally removed a crumpled piece of paper. "This was wedged inside."

It was a handwritten piece of paper torn from a notebook. Wilmer grabbed the page from Harriet's grasp. It was the missing page from Mr. Sneed's journal. He remembered reading, *But soon everyone will fear the name of—*

Now he could read the rest of the sentence:

Clarence Dillard Sneed!
After hundreds of dead mice, we have perfected the process. Now we're ready to move on to human brains! Our brainwashing frequency works best on kids. Twelve-year-old

brains are the perfect receptors
for our mind-altering procedure.
They have the fewest soupy side
effects.

At last, we can create our awe-
inspiring army of juvenile lackeys,
and take over the world! And
here's how . . .

With a shaky voice, Wilmer began to read
aloud. Roxie and Harriet stood next to him, their
jaws hanging open as they absorbed every terrible
word.

How to Erase a Brain
And have it obey your every
command!
By CD

Controlling the brain is simple
with these three steps: the Squeal,
the Trigger, and the Command!

1. The Squeal

My greatest discovery: a high-pitched squawk that wipes the brain of all thought. It also makes subjects angry and woozy, and then they want to gnaw on seat cushions and stuff. But you can't have everything.

Caution: a full-blast Squeal turns even adult brains into soup. And you don't want brain soup: It stains the carpeting.

2. The Trigger

We follow the Squeal with a single hypnotic phrase chosen carefully for its delicate balance of syllables. It primes the brain for the command. Otherwise, we just get a blank brain that makes our subject do nothing but stare and drool a bit.

3. The Command
This is the best part!

"That's horrible," said Wilmer. "But that's all the note says."

"Turn the page over," said Harriet.

"Oh, right. Thanks," mumbled Wilmer. He continued reading.

The Command is the part when we tell the brain exactly what to do, such as "Make me an omelet," or "Take over the world now." But if we go ordering kids to make omelets or take over worlds, some adults might overhear and get upset, or want their own omelets. So we use a Subliminal Message Muddler, yet another genius invention of mine.

Oh, I love my Muddler! I give horrible, evil orders, and the machine turns the words into happy, random pieces of advice! Twelve-year-old brains primed by the Squeal and Trigger will understand and follow my orders perfectly, while everyone else will think I'm being helpful.

Mwa-ha-ha!

I love writing that. I'll do it again!

Mwa-ha-ha! And an extra mwa-ha!

Soon our horribly sinister, heinous, repulsive, contemptible, and oh-so-wonderful army will help me take over the world. And no one will suspect a thing!

Boy, am I smart!

Wilmer looked up, his hands quivering. The plot was even more terrible than he had imagined.

Harriet leaned over and pointed to the page. "There's a note here in the margin." They squinted to read it:

The order must be precise, and the frequency exact. Soupy brains can't carry out our orders, but if all goes according to plan, we can keep brains from being soupy for days, even weeks. Maybe. I suppose we'll find out soon enough.

"Simply awful," muttered Harriet. She looked at Wilmer, her eyes misty.

Wilmer scanned the page again, looking for a clue on how to stop the twisted scheme, but found none.

"A Subliminal Message Muddler," Harriet mumbled. "I should have known. A subliminal message is a phrase that sounds like one thing, but your brain hears something different. It's sometimes used in music or advertising. It's very controversial science."

"Well, nothing can be much more controversial than building a machine to brainwash kids and take over the world," said Wilmer. Harriet and Roxie nodded in agreement.

Roxie pointed to a small orange button at the top of the console that flashed erratically and read SUBLIMINAL MESSAGE MUDDLER. "I was wondering what that did." She walked over to the board. "So if I tell the kids to do horrible things, the machine will spit out the opposite, right?" She spoke into the microphone. "Students, join my army and destroy the world." Then she pressed the orange button.

Her voice boomed back at them, screechy and echoey and metallic, so that it sounded nothing like Roxie's voice. Instead, it resembled the unrecognizable electronic distortions they had heard all weekend. "Kids, eat lots of grapefruit and love prancing ponies," sang the loudspeaker.

"I love ponies," said Wilmer. "And grapefruit is a great source of Vitamin C."

"So that explains why we've been hearing those weird messages," said Roxie with a shiver. "But we don't need to scramble *our* message. I'll just order kids to stop being brain-dead zombies, right?" She lowered her hand to press the console button and transmit a message to the entire hotel.

"Wait. It's not that simple," cautioned Harriet.

"Remember, there are three steps. The Command is just the final one. We have the Squeal, the Trigger, and then the Command. The Squeal empties their minds. Then the Trigger primes the brains for orders. Then, lastly, the Command tells them what to do."

"So we still need the frequency for the Squeal and the right words for the Trigger," said Roxie.

"Exactly," said Harriet.

Wilmer picked up a handful of papers and groaned. "But there are hundreds of frequencies on these pages and I can't make heads or tails out of any of them!" He flung the pages down on the table with frustration. One sheet teetered off the edge and floated to the ground. Wilmer picked the paper up. "Never mind. Here it is."

He held a sheet with spiky patterns that resembled cascading ocean waves, or maybe splashing soup. The page was titled, *Perfected brain-erasing frequency. Use with caution.* There were a number of settings for the radio console. On the very top of the page was a recipe for an egg-salad sandwich.

"Look!" exclaimed Wilmer, showing the page to Harriet.

"This is not the time to make egg salad," she said.

"No—below it!"

Harriet gasped. "'Perfected brain-erasing frequency'! That's it!" She gave Wilmer a kiss on the cheek, which Wilmer quickly wiped away. He thought he heard Roxie growl.

Harriet handed the paper to Roxie, who examined it and then fiddled with some knobs.

"We should record the sound," suggested Wilmer. "It might be of scientific value later. But first, cover your ears," he warned. "A full-blast Squeal is dangerous." He and Harriet put in their earplugs.

Roxie put on her headphones, rotated more knobs, and then pressed the red console button. A screechy distorted pitch shook the room . . . just as the door behind them swung open.

Roxie turned around, releasing the button in surprise. Elvira Padgett towered threateningly in the doorway, her mouth twisted into a sour scowl. Next to her stood Dr. Dill.

"What do you think you're doing?" Elvira rasped. "No one is allowed to touch this machine except Mr. Sneed. Oh, it hurts me so to see kids misbehaving. I think we need to pay Mr. Sneed a visit. Who knows what he'll do when he finds out about this?"

Wilmer gulped. He couldn't imagine what Mr. Sneed was capable of doing.

"You kids are in big trouble," warned Elvira.

"The biggest," agreed Dr. Dill.

CHAPTER TWENTY-THREE

How to Build an Exploding Volcano
By Dr. A. P. Swaghorn,
the Internet's Ultimate Authority
on Everything Science

Place a soda bottle straight up,
preferably on a piece of wood.
Use clay to shape a volcano base
around the bottle.
Fill the bottle most of the way
with warm water, red food
coloring, and a few drops of
dishwashing detergent.
Add 2 tablespoons baking soda.
Slowly pour in vinegar.
Stand back and watch your volcano
explode!

Tips:
• Don't aim your volcano at anyone.

- **Don't use Mentos and diet soda,
  or your volcano may cover the
  room with slime.**
- **And you don't want to cover the
  entire room with slime, right?**
- **Right?**

Standing in the exhibit hall, Claudius Dill stared in dismay at his broken volcano. All that work! He'd had visions of exploding green goop coating Wilmer Dooley. The volcano would spew fake lava high up in the air and directly down on his enemy.

But now? Now it would do nothing.

Claudius wasn't going to win first place in the science fair with a broken volcano on the floor. Of course, Wilmer Dooley couldn't win either, which meant it wasn't a total disaster.

But pretty much everything *else* was a total disaster, what with broken glass and puddles of chemicals covering the floor. Some strawberry-haired girl with thick glasses was starting to rise from the floor when a mouse ran over her shoe. She screamed and then fainted. Was that a leech on her arm?

Claudius was speechless. Who destroyed the exhibits? *He* hadn't done it. Neither had Vlad—they had been together all weekend, except for some quick bathroom breaks.

But who, then? Not Wilmer—the boy was a goody two-shoes through and through. That didn't stop Claudius from spreading lies about him, though. "Dooley destroyed this room!" he yelled to no one in particular. It made him feel good when he said bad things about Wilmer Dooley.

Claudius was surprised by the reactions from the other kids. They weren't just upset—they were *violently* upset. One kid, who had his foot in a cast, jumped up and down on his exhibit, kicking and screaming. A group of girls with matching yellow tank tops were yanking each other's hair. Other kids were hollering and punching the ground.

"Something isn't right," said Claudius to Vlad. "No one is acting very scientistlike."

Vlad scanned the room with a concerned frown. "Maybe. Yes. You're right. I hadn't noticed." He pointed to two girls who were nibbling on a chair. "That's something you don't see every day."

He scratched his chin. "But if *I* didn't destroy the exhibits, and *you* didn't . . . then someone else here is as conniving as us. Maybe even more so!"

Claudius gulped. He didn't like to think anyone could be more conniving than him. He scanned the room for suspicious-looking characters. But with all the students breaking things or yanking things or eating things, *everyone* seemed suspicious. A shiver crawled up Claudius's back.

"We should find Dooley," said Vlad. "He might know what's happening."

Claudius gave an annoyed grunt. "We can handle this ourselves."

A thin mouse of a boy ran past them, growled, and dove headfirst into the wall. Then he stood up, picked up a broken wooden beam, and gnawed at it while yelling, "Must mince meats!"

"Well, okay, I guess we can ask Dooley," said Claudius. "But we're *not* helping him become a hero again."

"Of course not," agreed Vlad. "But if you can't use a goody two-shoes to your own advantage, what's the point of having a goody two-shoes around at all?"

Claudius didn't think there *was* a point to having a goody two-shoes around at all, but he nodded and they walked out to find his sworn enemy.

In the radio control room, Elvira Padgett folded her arms. She looked stern and threatening and unhappy and vexed. Especially vexed.

"We've uncovered a horrible plot to create an army of evil middle-school scientists to take over the world!" shouted Roxie.

"Led by Mr. Sneed," added Wilmer.

Elvira stared at them, her eyes bulging. She crossed her arms even higher, so that they loomed over the kids and cast a shadow over their heads. "That's ridiculous. I've known Mr. Sneed for years. Why, he's always ending his PA announcements by telling everyone to be kind to rabbits and that sort of thing. He wouldn't create an army of middle-schoolers."

"Those are all subliminal messages," said

Harriet. "He's really telling kids to do evil things. It's just that he uses a machine to disguise the orders."

"Is it true?" gasped Dr. Dill. His face turned red with shock and anger. "That's dreadful! We need to take immediate action! Elvira, call the police! We must act now!" His Beethoven tone rang and he answered his phone. "Dr. Dill, here. I'm very busy and . . . What? A severe case of Herring Bone? . . . Yes, I see a pattern. . . ." He turned and walked out the door.

Elvira turned slowly back to the kids, her eyes narrowing. "That's a pretty incredible accusation."

"The proof is in all those pages," said Wilmer, pointing to the pile of papers spread over the table. "They even have Mr. Sneed's initials on them. I thought they stood for Claudius Dill, but I was wrong." He held up a piece of paper. "See? CD!"

"CD? That could stand for anything! Carnivorous Dinosaurs! Conniving Diapers! Congealed Doghouses!" Elvira straightened her back. She glowered at Wilmer. He took a step back, suddenly nervous.

But his worries quickly vanished when Elvira said, "If what you say is true, no one is safe. Follow me to my office." She looked at her watch. "The judging is about to start for the contest. But this is far more important. And there isn't much to judge anyway, I'm afraid."

"Does anyone know what happened to the exhibits?" asked Roxie.

"I'm afraid not. There are rumors of sabotage, of course." Elvira glanced at Wilmer. "We have suspects."

The kids followed her out of the room and down the hallway. They passed three boys in matching science goggles. One punched his hand against the wall, one rammed his head into a table, and one jabbed his nose at a lamp. Each act of violence sent shivers up Wilmer's spine, but it also filled his head with the urge to join in.

Wilmer bit his lip as they walked into Elvira's office. It was located right off the main lobby and behind the check-in counter. The floor of her office was piled high with stacks of books. Wilmer glanced at the titles. They were science textbooks.

They seemed to be about sound waves and physics. But Elvira wasn't a scientist.

Seated behind her large wooden desk, his feet up, was Mr. Sneed. He whistled.

"It's him!" cried Wilmer. "Get him! Stop him! Tie him up!"

"The kids seem to think you're hatching some sort of horrible plan to take over the world," said Elvira grimly.

"Oh, it's not me who hatched that plan," said Mr. Sneed with a short cackle.

Elvira closed her office door and locked it behind her. "No, quite right. It was me."

CHAPTER TWENTY-FOUR

Ms. Elvira Padgett,
  Our records show that the following
books are overdue from the library.
Please return them to avoid continued
fines.

- *Sound Frequencies for Dummies*
- *Structural Vibrations,
  Electromagnetic Wave Radiation, and
  other Scientific Sound Thingies*
- *Everything You Always Wanted to Know
  About Conquering the World but Were
  Afraid to Ask*
- *My Life in Mah-Jongg* by Valveeta
  Padgett
- *A Physical Exploration of the
  Attenuation of Sound Waves and Their
  Effect on Gray Matter and . . . Oh,
  Who Would Read This? I'm Bored Even
  Writing the Title*
- *Alexander the Great: The Toddler
  Years*
- *How to Build a Thousand-Foot Radio
  Tower by Yourself*
- *500 Recipes for Soup*

Harriet, Roxie, and Wilmer huddled together, knees quaking, as the two scheming adults snarled at them. "But you seemed so nice!" screamed Harriet to Elvira. "I mean, when you weren't pulling wings off flies and stuff. You can't be the one behind all of this."

"Of course it was me!" Elvira barked. She stepped closer. "World domination has been my lifelong dream."

"Mine too," said Mr. Sneed, rising from his chair. He smiled warmly at Elvira. "We have so much in common. Two peas in a pod. Two scoops on a cone. Two maggots eating a carcass."

"You're sweet," Elvira said, blushing. "When we stumbled upon evil sound frequencies, our plans were modest. We would turn brains into sloppy joes! Or a garden salad! But then we found a pitch that could control human brains *and* turn them into soup. The perfect way to raise an army! And serve lunch in a pinch. We just needed some kids to test it on. The state science fair was perfect. So many brains, big and juicy." She cackled three times, with Mr. Sneed joining her on the last one. "The last piece of the puzzle was to build a radio tower so we could project our announcements even louder."

"The final step in our master plan." Mr. Sneed giggled.

"The final step in our first step," Elvira corrected him. "Then we have additional first and final steps as we spread our brainwashing across the globe."

Mr. Sneed nodded. "You're always a step ahead of me."

"I *thought* the tower was part of the plan!" exclaimed Wilmer. "I found freshly buried wires, so I knew something must be up." He scratched his head. "But then, I assumed the tower was really old. I even saw cracks along the steel base."

Mr. Sneed sniffed. "You try building a nearly one-thousand-foot-tall metal tower by yourself over a weekend, and see how *you* do. Although it does seem to be falling apart quicker than I thought it would."

"But you can't take over the world!" cried Roxie. "You could never build enough radio towers to fill it."

Mr. Sneed shuddered. "I don't have enough wire."

"Of course not," spat Elvira. "We need something smaller. More effective. Something that kids everywhere listen to time and time again."

"Like an iNoise!" screamed Wilmer and Harriet at once.

Elvira smiled. She pulled a large cardboard box out from under her desk. It was the same box the kids had filled with their electronics on the first day they arrived. Elvira reached her hand inside and pulled out an iNoise. "Each is now designed to play a nearly silent, evil brain-warping frequency while dispensing our rotten commands. It's the perfect way to reach middle-school ears! But that's not the best part. Our sound app will automatically spread to other iNoises, like bacteria! Soon every iNoise in the world will become our own personal brainwashing device!"

Wilmer shuddered. He was all too familiar with bacteria and how easily they spread if unstopped. The Mumpley contagion had nearly made everyone in his school explode. But this was worse. *This* contagion might turn the world's brains into soup.

"We should go transmit our orders from the tower," said Elvira to Mr. Sneed.

"But what should we do with *them*?" Mr. Sneed pointed to Wilmer and his friends. His voice dripped in disgust.

Elvira shook her head. "Leave them here. Once we perform the final brain purge, they'll be part of our army."

"Wasting a mind is a terrible thing to waste," agreed Mr. Sneed. He hoisted the giant box of gadgets, cackled, and walked out the door with Elvira.

"Good-bye," said Elvira with a snort. "More like bad-bye, actually. Not much good about it. For you, at least."

She laughed again, as did Mr. Sneed. They closed the door behind them. Wilmer looked at Harriet and Roxie. He gulped. He took a deep breath and rushed to the door to break free.

It was locked.

He kicked it as hard as he could.

And stubbed his toe.

He rammed into it with his shoulder.

Which really hurt his shoulder.

He started to run into it headfirst, and then decided that was a bad idea.

It was no use. They were trapped.

A small loudspeaker was fixed above Elvira's desk. It squawked. Roxie clamped on her headphones, and Wilmer and Harriet flipped in their earplugs.

Still, the blaring announcement trickled into Wilmer's ears. His head spun. He balled his fists and tried his best to bury the brainwashed fury that was starting to bubble up inside him. He needed to stay in control of his brain, now more than ever.

"Attention, dear, dear students," said the raspy, distorted voice of Mr. Sneed. Or maybe Elvira. It was impossible to tell. "Happy, happy, joy, joy, fun, fun. Thank you."

"Oh, no!" exclaimed Harriet. "More evil orders!"

The loudspeaker screeched and the walls creaked. The floor trembled. The cracks in the drywall—for they were everywhere—now looked even deeper. One long crevice reached from the floorboards all the way to the ceiling. Some drywall flakes crumbled to the ground.

Roxie pounded on the door. "Help! We're trapped!"

Wilmer and Harriet joined her. "Help! Help! Let us out!"

After a minute, they stopped hitting. Wilmer's palms hurt and it wasn't getting them anywhere, anyway. "It's no use!" wailed Roxie. "We'll never escape."

Wilmer crumpled to the floor like the plaster floating down from the ceiling. He buried his head in his hands. "Observation!" he moaned. "That's what scientists do, and I've done a lousy job of it. I failed to observe Elvira being evil. I didn't observe Mr. Sneed wiring the radio tower, even though he was walking around with cables sticking out of his back pocket. I insisted Claudius was guilty, even when it was impossible. And now we're all going to suffer the consequences."

"Don't be so hard on yourself." Harriet sat beside Wilmer and put her arm around his shoulders. "You're cute when you're angry. And it's not your fault we're in this predicament. Only sort of."

"And I don't totally blame you for acting like a jerk the last day or two," said Roxie. "Only mostly."

"Thanks, I think," mumbled Wilmer. "But we all know I'm the reason every middle-schooler in the world will soon have soup for brains."

"It's not so bad," said Roxie. "I like soup." Wilmer and Harriet frowned. "Well, I guess it is so bad. It can't be much worse, actually. But I missed all the signs too. I'm a reporter! Gwendolyn Bray would have figured it out."

"And I'm a scientist too," said Harriet. "Not as great as you, Wilmy. I *am* a Grand Newtonian winner, but I don't pretend to be as amazing as you, not in the least. Just this morning a girl stole my calculator and chewed on it. I thought she was hungry."

But Wilmer knew he was the most responsible. He swallowed a big gob of guilt-laden spittle, and then the door opened.

CHAPTER TWENTY-FIVE

The Private Office of Elvira Padgett
Restricted!
Go away!
Do not enter without knocking, and
even then, don't even think about it!
Keep out!
That means you, buster!

Mrs. Valveeta Padgett gasped with surprise. Her gasp was followed by a slight wheeze. She rested her hand over her heart. There were children in her sister's office. She hadn't expected that. And certainly not *these* children. Why did Wilmer Dooley seem to pop up everywhere? Mrs. Padgett would have nightmares for weeks, with Wilmer Dooley jumping in and out of them like some sort of deranged jack-in-the-box.

Elvira had told her not to enter this office, and she was very particular about that sort of thing. But Mrs. Padgett needed a quiet place to work.

Exceptions must be made. After all, she'd just had a brilliant idea for her next television script, comparing mah-jongg to tree fungus. You might not think the two have much in common. Actually, you'd be right. That's why she needed a quiet place to work.

She would have written in her hotel room—she had her own king-size suite. But the faucet leaked and the steady *drip, drip, drip* was driving her nuts. This whole hotel was falling apart, actually. What did Mr. Sneed do, anyway? He wasn't much of a handyman, that much was for sure.

"I'll leave you kids alone . . . ," Mrs. Padgett said as she stepped back and began to close the door.

But Wilmer jumped up, waving his hands. What did that irritating boy want now? "Wait! Stop!" he cried. "We're trapped. Your sister and Mr. Sneed are planning to take over the world! They're brainwashing all the kids and turning their brains into soupy mush. Or mushy soup. Really, it's the same thing."

Mrs. Padgett frowned. She didn't want to believe Wilmer Dooley. The boy was prone to raising needless alarms. But she had to admit: that was *so* like Elvira. As kids, Elvira always said her dream in life was to become an astronaut or to turn people's heads into mush. And she hadn't become an astronaut, had she?

Mrs. Padgett looked up. A loud rumbling sound came from above her.

She jumped to the side—pure instinct, really— as part of the roof collapsed, sending plaster and rubble and a large wooden beam crashing into the room. It missed her by inches. A cloud of dust settled around her legs. She'd have to repolish her shoes now, which was a shame. She had spent a great chunk of the morning polishing them already. "Oh, my. Is my sister destroying the hotel, too?"

"I don't know," admitted Wilmer. "But the shifting and cracking walls don't look safe."

No, they didn't. Mrs. Padgett had noticed, of course. Science was about observation and being a television star. Mostly, being a star. But a little observation was necessary. She figured the crevices and uneven ceilings were just part of the decor, or that they were due to Mr. Sneed's inadequate maintenance. She hadn't considered that they might be part of some diabolical scheme.

"We'd better find your sister and Mr. Sneed," said Wilmer.

"Don't be absurd," said Mrs. Padgett. "I can't let you leave." Mrs. Padgett didn't support her sister's insane thirst for power. But family *was* family.

"You have to," pleaded Harriet. "Or the entire world is doomed."

"Surely you exaggerate," said Mrs. Padgett. "Doomed? That's so melodramatic. A few kids' heads turn into soup. Is that so bad? Do you dislike soup? And maybe the world should be conquered. Have you considered that?"

"They'd probably cancel your TV show," said Roxie. "There won't be television shows if everyone's brains are turned to mush."

Mrs. Padgett shrieked. Saving the world wasn't worth her efforts—but saving her TV show? She had worked too hard to see it canceled merely because her sister wanted brain soup. What about that script she wrote comparing mah-jongg with plumbing? Was her Emmy just a pipe dream?

"Very well," Mrs. Padgett said, stepping aside. "Save the world then. If you must."

Wilmer, Harriet, and Roxie rushed out of the office. As they scooted past the registration counter and into the lobby, they nearly crashed into Dr. Dill.

"Dr. Dill!" cried Roxie. "Mr. Sneed and—"

"Whatever it is, I'm sure it's horrible and needs my immediate attention to save hundreds of kids. But I should take this first." His phone was blaring Beethoven. "Dill, here . . . She has Sticky Buns, you say? . . . Have you tried icing them?" He wandered away.

Wilmer raced down the hallway, with Roxie and Harriet following. They needed to get back to the radio control room. They needed to order everyone to cover their ears.

The hallway was dense with students, all of them performing random acts of mayhem. Some ripped apart the couch, and others clawed at the walls. A few girls in JUNIOR HIGH COLLEGE TECH PREP FOR REALLY GIFTED SMART KIDS jackets barked like angry wolves.

One girl in a dress held a knife and was covered in blood!

Wilmer screamed!

No, wait. She was covered in pizza sauce and she held a plastic spoon. But still, it was frightening.

Wilmer sidestepped the lumbering kids as they snarled at him and his friends. A few trudged toward them, but they were pretty easy to avoid. Up ahead was Ernie. Wilmer's best friend wandered the hall in a daze, stumbling forward and throwing random punches at the air. "Ernie!" Wilmer yelled. "Are you okay? We have to save the world!"

Ernie stared at Wilmer, his eyes narrowed into angry slits. He hissed.

"Ernie!" yelled Wilmer. "It's me!"

Ernie hissed again.

Wilmer grabbed Ernie's shoulders and looked deeply into his eyes. Deep down, below the anger, was good old Ernie. If only Wilmer could get through to him, and peel back the force that was twisting his mind. "Snap out of it, buddy. You can do it." Wilmer held up his thumb. "Give me your best-friend thumbshake!"

Ernie looked down at Wilmer's thumb and then at his own thumb. Was that a glimmer of recognition in his eye? Ernie held his thumb up. He brought it closer to Wilmer's thumb.

Closer.

Then he lunged and poked at Wilmer's eye. Thankfully, Wilmer wore glasses.

But Wilmer was unprepared for Ernie's sudden attack. Ernie's hands clutched Wilmer's throat as he ranted, "Must choke collars! Must hit records! Must whip cream!" Wilmer fell to the ground and Ernie landed on top of him. Ernie's fingers clutched tighter.

And then a hand flew down and clocked Ernie on the nose.

Ernie fell off, knocked out cold.

Harriet massaged her knuckles. "That hurt a bit more than I expected. But by taking into account the mathematical formula of $F=ma$, where F is force and ma stands for mass times acceleration, I was able to aim about one hundred Newtons of force directly at Ernie's proboscis and . . ."

"Um, maybe we can finish that later," suggested Wilmer. "We're in a bit of a rush."

"Anything for you, Wilmy," Harriet answered shyly, with a bat of her eyes.

They dashed down the hall. There it was: the door to the control room. The door was open— Harriet didn't even need to whistle! Wilmer peeked inside. He took a step past the doorframe.

And then the roof collapsed.

Wilmer leaped back, narrowly avoiding huge hunks of plaster and a few steel beams as they crashed to the ground. A toilet from the room above fell through the center table, followed by pipes and a sink. Part of a bed slid into the room, and an end table. Dust and pulverized rubble swirled through the air and covered the kids. Harsh coughs bellowed from Wilmer's throat.

When the dust cleared, Wilmer stared in dismay. Every piece of equipment was completely destroyed. Small flames leaped from the counter, wires sparked, and a layer of thin plaster covered everything. A fallen piece of concrete had created a giant crater in the middle of the audio controls. The furniture from the room directly overhead lay in pieces on the ground.

Wilmer bent down and ran his fingers along one of the steel beams that had collapsed. It was lined with cracks. It reminded him of the strangely worn radio tower.

"So that's it?" cried Roxie. "We've lost? The bad guys got away? The kids are brainwashed and the only way to reverse the evil orders has been destroyed?" Her cheeks were moist with tears. She stepped closer to Wilmer. She gazed into his eyes. "If this is the end of the road, I guess I should tell you something. Wilmer, I've felt this way for a long time. I've never had the nerve to tell you but I have always—"

"This is *not* the end of the road," interrupted Harriet. She stepped directly in front of Wilmer. She stood only an inch from him, maybe less— Wilmer didn't have time to accurately measure the distance. "Maybe we can still save everyone. Mr. Sneed and Elvira are heading to the radio tower for the final brain purge. We have to go there. Now. And stop them!"

"Um, how about after Roxie finishes what she was about to say?" suggested Wilmer. His heart was beating rapidly and his adrenal glands were pumping, secreting buckets of dopamine and epinephrine. "Go on," He nudged Harriet a few inches to the side so he could better stare at Roxie.

"There's no time," Roxie said. "Harriet is right. We have to find Elvira and Mr. Sneed *now*. Everything else can wait."

Wilmer groaned, but nodded. Roxie was probably just going to say, "I have always wanted to bowl." Or, "I have always liked applesauce."

They sprinted down the hall. Fissures spread throughout the ceiling above, and small avalanches of plaster rained down. They could hear unsettling creaks from the walls and beneath their feet. Wilmer sidestepped growling and snarling kids who didn't seem to notice the hotel's state of disaster. "Must crack corn!" one roared. "Must crunch numbers!"

Wilmer and his friends reached the lobby and found themselves standing in the middle of a riot. Kids smashed chairs against walls and pieces of wall against chairs. Loose flooring was torn up, and roofing was torn down. To make matters worse,

Claudius and Vlad were running toward them. Wilmer crouched, ready for anything.

"What's happening?" asked Vlad, looking around the lobby in horror. "Everyone's gone completely crazy!"

"Do you see any brain mush?" asked Wilmer, his legs shaking with worry. Vlad shook his head. Wilmer took a deep breath. "Then there's still time."

"All the kids are being brainwashed into helping Elvira and Mr. Sneed rule the world," explained Roxie. "If we don't stop them, everyone's brains will be turned into soup."

"Cool," said Claudius. When Wilmer shot him a dirty look, he quickly added, "Or rather, it would be cool, if they weren't planning on turning *our* brains into soup too."

"Maybe we can help stop them," offered Vlad.

"We'll take all the help we can get," said Roxie.

"How do we know they aren't in league with Sneed and Elvira?" Wilmer pointed to the cousins with an accusing finger. His voice shook with anger. They were still the enemy! "Harriet and I have been wearing earplugs. Roxie has her earphones. But if they're so innocent, then why aren't *they* acting nuts? Huh? You can never fool observation, and I've observed their suspicious behavior all weekend!"

Vlad tugged his earlobe and wiggled his finger. After a moment, he extracted a small button-size device hidden in his ear. "Spy buds," he said.

Claudius removed two from his own ears. "Pretty cool, huh? They let us listen in on conversations. We've been trying to learn secrets, especially about the science fair. Anything to get an edge. These suckers can hear conversations from across the room."

"But wouldn't that make the announcements louder?" asked Roxie.

"A lot louder. So every time they made an announcement, we had to turn the volume way down so we couldn't hear anything," explained Claudius. He tugged his earlobe to show how the volume control worked.

"We've learned all kinds of stuff," said Vlad. "We overheard six school locker combinations. We learned about three surprise parties. And we know what brand of toothpaste that group of girls from the Biotechnical Educational Institute for Kids Who Are Smarter Than You brush with."

"No one really talked about anything helpful," Claudius admitted.

"You must have at least overheard Sneed and Elvira plotting!" exclaimed Wilmer.

Claudius shook his head. "We never listen in on adult conversations. What's the fun in that?"

"We're wasting time," interrupted Roxie. "We have to save the world! Come on!"

While running to the doors, Wilmer kept glancing at the cousins. He bit his lip. He couldn't believe that, once again, he was teaming up with his sworn enemy. But Wilmer swallowed his pride and followed the group of would-be world-savers out of the hotel.

CHAPTER TWENTY-SIX

SAC À PUCES PALLADIUM, LODGE, AND RESORTLIKE HOTEL

About the Hotel

The Sac à Puces was built in 1928 by a group of Canadian immigrants who took a wrong turn on the way to Alaska. A very wrong turn. But the men in the group didn't want to stop and ask for directions, so they stayed and built a hotel instead. Many felt a hotel in the middle of nowhere, miles from civilization, would struggle to find guests. They were right. Most of the guests who come here take wrong turns going somewhere else, don't like to ask for directions, and so decide to stay.

The hotel was completely renovated this past year in anticipation of the 45th Annual State Science Fair and Consortium. The old wood supports were replaced by shiny steel

beams, installed by our own handy Mr. Sneed.
A new loudspeaker system and radio tower
were built to amplify our announcements.
And ~~brainwashing devices~~ *new drapes were*
installed.

Some of the students had wandered onto the hotel grounds and were beating bushes and terrorizing trees.

"Once Mr. Sneed and Elvira issue their final announcement, it'll be too late to save them," said Roxie as she surveyed the chaos.

"This would have been a much better science project than our volcano," said Vlad. "Maybe next year?" He and Claudius exchanged high fives.

"Can you please keep your plans for world domination to yourselves?" said Wilmer testily. "At least until we stop *this* plan for world domination?"

The five of them rushed across the lawn and into the woods. The radio tower was easy to spot, since it rose high over the tree line. But once they were within the forest, the leaves obscured their view.

"Which way?" asked Claudius. "Do we look at tree moss for directions?"

"That doesn't work," said Wilmer. "Just follow the wires." He pointed to the exposed cords still lying on the ground from when Wilmer had pulled them up the night before. "But be careful of tree roots and stuff. I can make a splint if you need one, but it takes time."

They ran, Harriet in the lead and Wilmer at the back. Wilmer almost tripped a few times, but they all managed to avoid twisted ankles and skinned knees. After a few minutes Roxie yelled, "There they are!"

Sure enough, a slight hole in the canopy of leaves revealed the enormous tower. Two small figures scampered up the endless flights of stairs. Mr. Sneed and Elvira! Even from far away, Wilmer was sure it was them.

Just looking at them makes me so angry!

Wilmer gulped. He needed his full wits about him if he was going to stop this scheme. He pushed his anger down and took a deep breath, and soon they reached the tall steel structure. Stairs went up and up and up, with dozens of landings. A lone ladder was the only way to climb the final hundred feet to a platform at the very top. Mr. Sneed and Elvira had already reached it. It looked dangerous; one slip would send them hurtling to the ground. For a moment, Wilmer had second thoughts about following them. But this wasn't the time for queasiness. "Hurry!"

"I think I'll wait down here," muttered Claudius, his face turning green. He looked up, seemed to grow dizzy, and then looked back down and kicked a rock.

"You're not scared of heights, are you?" asked Wilmer.

"Um, m-maybe?" stuttered Claudius.

"I'll keep him company," said Vlad. "Besides, I don't want to scuff my shoes." Vlad pointed down at his black wingtips, then adjusted his bow tie.

"Are you scared of heights too?" asked Wilmer.

Vlad pulled at his collar, a bead of sweat dripping from his neck. "No, but Mr. Sneed is pretty big, right? How do you plan on stopping him?"

Wilmer hadn't thought about that. But he couldn't sit back and do nothing—even if, now that he thought about it, Mr. Sneed would probably just toss Wilmer off the side of the tower.

"We'll stop them in the name of science!" Wilmer declared. "We'll stop them with brain power!"

"That sounds pretty wimpy," said Vlad. "I think I'll stay down here and keep an eye on Claudius if you don't mind, thank you."

Wilmer bounded up the stairs, two steps at time. Roxie and Harriet followed. The tower was in even worse shape than Wilmer had thought. Cracks lined the metal floor. Fissures spread across the rails and beams. A few screws spun off their supports and bounced along the ground. Mr. Sneed was definitely not a skilled radio-tower builder. How sturdy was this thing? Wilmer continued racing up the stairs, but with each step the metal seemed to groan and shift beneath him.

Soon Wilmer was panting. His calves burned.

Usually, Wilmer's only exercise was from twisting microscope knobs. That meant he had very strong fingertips, but his stair-climbing skills were weak. He ignored his shortage of breath as best he could. He couldn't dawdle—not when every extra second brought Mr. Sneed and Elvira closer to making that final, dreaded announcement.

Well, maybe he could dawdle a little. Just for a few seconds. Ten seconds. A couple more. Okay, now back to climbing!

The stairs ended. Wilmer grasped the ladder attached to the tower exterior. He put his foot onto the bottom rung. One big wind gust would send him hurtling to certain death. Well, science wasn't for the weak-kneed. It was about intellect! Cunning! And good calves, apparently.

He pulled himself up one rung. And then another. Up and up.

"This . . . is . . . exhausting," said Wilmer, but he said it with considerable panting, so that it sounded more like "This . . . *pant, pant, pant* . . . is . . . *pant, pant, pant* . . . exhaust . . . *pant, pant, pant* . . . ing."

"But we can't stop! Too much is at stake,"

shouted Roxie, who didn't seem nearly as out of breath as Wilmer.

"Faster, you guys!" cried Harriet. She didn't sound tired at all.

Wilmer bit his lip and kept on scaling.

Finally, after what seemed like forever, they reached the very top of the ladder. Wilmer practically fell off the final step and onto the grated metal floor of the platform, gasping.

Mr. Sneed and Elvira stood next to an audio control board. While much smaller than the one in the hotel, it was still fairly impressive, with dozens of knobs, a microphone, and a monitor that displayed sound patterns. Wilmer wondered how they had lugged it all the way up here.

"We've . . . ," said Wilmer, still panting, ". . . come . . . to . . ." He put his hands on his knees and wheezed.

"You've come to what?" asked Elvira.

Wilmer raised his hand. "One second . . . ," he pleaded as he fought for air. Finally he blurted out between pants, "We've come . . . to stop . . . you."

Elvira laughed. So did Mr. Sneed, who didn't

even glance at Wilmer as he continued twisting knobs on the control panel. "*You* stop *me*?" he said. "Ha! I'm twice your size, you know."

"Well, yes," admitted Wilmer. "But I've got brain power!" He winced. That really *did* sound wimpy, he realized.

"He'll stop you because he's Wilmer Dooley!" shouted Harriet, stepping forward and jabbing her fist in the air. "The most amazing kid scientist ever. You'll be sorry you messed with him."

"Um, maybe you can keep that down," whispered Wilmer. "No sense bragging."

"How about I just throw you off the tower?" snarled Mr. Sneed. He puffed out his chest and rolled up his sleeve as he flexed his enormous arms, engorged veins etched on his muscles.

"I was afraid you'd suggest that," whimpered Wilmer.

"Show him *your* biceps, Wilmy!" shouted Harriet, pushing him forward.

"Um, no thanks." Wilmer squirmed.

Mr. Sneed snarled, "We're ready to transmit, my dear."

"Wonderful!" Elvira let out a loud cackle. "One transmission and all the kids at the hotel will be under our control forever! Or at least until their brains turn soupy." She pointed to Wilmer and his friends. "They annoy me. Toss them off the side."

"With pleasure." Mr. Sneed laughed.

Roxie still had her tape recorder strapped around her shoulder. She put her headphones over her ears and yanked the plug from its socket. "I don't think so!" she howled.

"This isn't the time for an interview," whispered Wilmer.

"I've got this," answered Roxie. "No need for the Subliminal Message Muddler now." She pressed the play button. A loud crackle erupted from the machine. Harriet and Wilmer wedged their earplugs into place as Roxie twisted the tape recorder volume up to its highest level. The Squeal she had recorded in the audio control room blared with its full brainwashing power.

"You will end your mean tricks!" she yelled. "You will let us go and stop what you're doing!"

Mr. Sneed hooted. "That won't work on us! You

need to say the Trigger first. And you don't know what it is."

Squeal, Trigger, Command. That was the exact order. They needed the Trigger, the key phrase that put brains into a hypnotic state.

Mr. Sneed stepped closer. "I think it's time we threw you kids off the tower."

Wilmer thought back. Science was about observation. What had he observed? What was the Trigger?

Mr. Sneed grabbed Wilmer by the collar. It was impressive how easily he lifted him. Wilmer might have admired the man's strength if he didn't think he was going to die in about four seconds.

Unless . . .

Of course!

Every announcement that weekend had begun with the exact same words! They must be the Trigger.

"Attention, dear, dear students!" screamed Wilmer as Mr. Sneed carted him to the railing. Wilmer's voice rose over the screeching drone of

Roxie's tape recorder. "I said, '*Attention, dear, dear students!*'"

Mr. Sneed froze. He still held Wilmer over his head, which was rather uncomfortable for Wilmer. But Mr. Sneed wasn't tossing him over the railing, so he wasn't about to complain.

"You will stop your mean tricks," Wilmer ordered. "You will become good people! You will stop trying to take over the world! And . . . and . . . love unicorns and rainbows." He shrugged. "I mean, it's hard to be mean if you love unicorns and rainbows, right? Oh, and can you put me down, please?"

Roxie turned off her tape recorder as Mr. Sneed slowly lowered Wilmer. The man stared blankly forward. A bit of drool fell from his lips. "Must love unicorns," Mr. Sneed muttered.

"Must fill world with rainbows," Elvira mumbled.

The two stepped forward in unison, their menace dissolved like hot cocoa powder in a steaming mug of milk. They lowered themselves onto the ladder and began to climb down from the tower. Blank smiles radiated from their otherwise vacant faces.

They left a small trail of soupy brain behind them, dripping from their ears.

"I love rainbows," muttered Elvira.

"Unicorns are my friends," mumbled Mr. Sneed.

"That worked surprisingly well," said Wilmer. Then to Roxie he said, "I think it's time you gave the best *Mumpley Musings* broadcast ever."

CHAPTER TWENTY-SEVEN

How to Build a Thousand-Foot
Radio Tower by Yourself
- Get twenty-five tons of sheet
  metal
- Learn how to weld
- Use lots of wire
- Be careful of cracks in the
  support beams, and loose screws
- Cross your fingers. I mean,
  come on. You're going to build
  a thousand-foot radio tower by
  yourself? Are you crazy?

It was a fairly standard soundboard, and Roxie was an expert. She adjusted a few knobs, tweaked a few dials, and then leaned into the microphone. A high-pitched squeak erupted, the sound bouncing off the trees and echoing across the property.

Wilmer felt his head becoming cloudy as the voice reverberated inside his skull.

"Attention, dear, dear students," said Roxie. "You will all go back to being normal now, and you will never listen to orders to join a brainwashed army and take over the world ever again."

Roxie lifted her finger from the board. Wilmer's brain cleared. The sense of anger that had been swirling inside him the last couple of days was gone. A peaceful silence filled the air. A satisfying calm swam through Wilmer's brain.

"Do you think that did it?" asked Roxie.

Wilmer nodded.

Harriet pointed. "Look!"

They were so high up on the tower that they could see over the tree line and all the way to the small figures wandering out onto the hotel grounds. Kids shook hands. Two boys danced. A group of girls hugged. No one kicked bushes or hit flowers. No one punched the air.

"We did it!" exclaimed Harriet. She held out her arms, waiting for Wilmer to hug her.

Wilmer wanted to embrace Roxie, not Harriet.

He yearned to look deeply into his love's eyes and say suave, clever things.

Instead, he looked away and coughed awkwardly.

Suddenly, a loud metallic crack reverberated from above. The tip of the tower directly over them snapped. The metal antenna, now a dangerous twenty-foot spike of death, smashed into a beam above them, bounced off, and then plummeted one thousand feet to the ground.

It landed, spike down, only a foot from Claudius below.

"What happened?" asked Harriet.

Loose screws. Cracks.

Wilmer had assumed they had formed because the tower was poorly built, just like the hotel. But what if there were another factor? The realization shocked him. "Sound waves!" he shouted. "Harriet, I'm no expert, but do you think the high-pitched Squeals from the announcements are part of the reason the tower is fracturing? And why the hotel is falling apart too?"

Harriet looked up, thinking. "If the metal was

already weak, and a sound wave hit just the right frequency, and caused just the right vibrations, it could split metal. In theory, yes. But I doubt that could actually happen—"

The platform under their feet snapped. The metal grating fractured. The cracks grew and spread like manic, evil eels, swimming through the floor and up the metal beams.

"Okay, maybe it could happen," Harriet admitted.

"Let's get out of here!" yelled Wilmer.

They scrambled over the railing and down the ladder. Harriet went first, then Roxie, and finally Wilmer. Just as Wilmer grabbed the top rung, he heard a violent smashing of metal, and the platform above him collapsed. The control panel and computer plummeted to the ground. Wilmer ducked as a large chunk of metal skidded across the deck and over the side, narrowly missing his head.

"Faster!" yelled Wilmer. Beams cracked as they raced down the ladder. With a deafening snap, the top railing of the tower broke off. The metal clasps

that were holding the ladder split. There was nothing mooring it except for a single metal clip on the
very bottom.

It was scary enough climbing down the side
of a tower, where one slip would mean immediate
death. But climbing down a wildly swaying ladder while screws and metal shards plummeted past
was much more frightening. Roxie and Harriet
hurled themselves off the final rung and onto the
metal staircase. The ladder fell backward. Wilmer
jumped. For a moment he was in midair, grasping
at nothing, his arms flailing. But then the tips of his
fingers grazed the platform railings. He dug in with
his outstretched digits.

He thanked his microscope-twisting for his
superstrong fingertips.

He pulled himself up and onto the platform.
But the metal walls were still fracturing around
them. The cracks in the floor were spreading like
quickly growing vines.

They clambered onto the stairs: down a flight,
across the next platform, and then down another

flight. There were hundreds, maybe thousands of steps. Each brought them closer to the ground, but they still had so far to go!

Then the entire tower shuddered, as if the supports below had shifted or perhaps had grown angry at all the climbing. The staircase ripped from its position, tearing completely off the structure. The metal beneath them sheared in half. The platform quivered to the left while the steps leaped to the right.

"Jump!" yelled Wilmer.

Harriet leaped from the staircase and fell onto the platform below. But as she landed, the floor moaned and shifted even more to the left, and the stairs fell more to the right. There was a large empty gap of space between them. A poor jump would mean plummeting like the metal hunks that fell around them.

"Roxie! Go!" cried Wilmer.

Roxie leaped across the crevice. It was a good jump—Wilmer remembered that Roxie had won the school long-jump competition in fourth grade—and she landed solidly on the platform. But it shifted under her weight, clanking loudly as the floor inclined a few feet farther. The platform was now steeply angled, and both Roxie and Harriet had to cling to the grating to keep from sliding off. The staircase fell farther from them, with Wilmer still on it.

"Come on, Wilmer!" cried Roxie. "You can do it! Jump!"

He could. Just barely. Maybe. He wasn't a good jumper. He had entered that same fourth-grade long-jump competition as Roxie, coming in forty-fourth out of forty-five. But he needed to try.

The platform slipped again. Wilmer feared it was about to plummet to the ground, with Harriet and Roxie on top of it. But it only plunged a few feet before wedging itself onto a bent steel support beam and stopping.

That was the good news. But it was otherwise bad news for Wilmer. The platform was now too far for him to jump to. He'd never make it, even if he hadn't come in forty-fourth place in fourth-grade long jumping. "Go ahead," he yelped. He remembered Ernie's heroic gesture the night before. "Save yourselves."

"No! Leap!" yelled Harriet. "You can make it!"

"You really think so?" asked Wilmer.

Harriet shook her head. "No, you don't have a chance, actually." Tears ran down her cheeks. Her voice was choked with emotion. "I'll always remember you, Wilmy! My precious Wilmy! We would have had such lovely, smart children!"

CHAPTER TWENTY-EIGHT

A Physical Exploration of the
Attenuation of Sound Waves and Their Effect on
Gray Matter and . . . Oh, Who Would Read This?
I'm Bored Even Writing the Title.
By Dr. Persnickel Horowitz

Think of water waves, one after another after another. Wait, I'm getting seasick just writing about them. Hold on. . . . Deep breath.

Okay. I feel better.

Sound waves are like that, which is why I always wear a life preserver when studying them. We can't hear the gaps between the waves, because they come at us too frequently. That's why we call it "frequency" and not "slow wave gap things"!

The closer the waves are to each other, the higher the sound.

Did you know that dogs hear higher frequencies than humans? They can detect sounds we can't. So when dogs tell jokes, they usually bark them at really high frequencies, so only their dog friends can hear them.

Opera stars have been known to shatter glass with their singing. In theory, those same vibrations could shatter metal! Sound waves at the right frequency and volume can make glass vibrate faster and faster until it breaks. So never invite an opera singer over for dinner. Or put the nice china in the basement first.

Did you know that after the age of twenty years old, people lose some ability to hear ultrahigh pitches, meaning children are more susceptible to certain sounds than adults? That's good to know if you want to brainwash them!

Vlad picked at his cuticles while Claudius scowled at him. Claudius had never pegged his cousin for a coward before. Vlad said he stayed behind to look after him. Baloney! Vlad hadn't looked at Claudius once since Wilmer scaled the tower. Vlad's knees were shaking, too. His face was green.

At least Claudius had a good reason for his own shaking knees: he was scared of heights, and being scared of heights was serious stuff. Height was the only thing Claudius feared! Well, not including spiders, assorted monsters, the dark, and being electrocuted by a fallen power line.

Claudius had other reasons to stay where he was too, and they had nothing to do with his fear of heights. He couldn't help Wilmer *again*! Assisting him when he cured that colorful contagion had been a big mistake. If Claudius turned into a soup-brained army drone, so be it. At least Wilmer would suffer the same fate.

Unless Wilmer succeeded. What if Dooley *did* stop Mr. Sneed and Elvira and become a hero one more time? Could Claudius let him take all the glory *again*?

Never!

But Wilmer couldn't succeed. Mr. Sneed was too strong.

Then Roxie's announcement soared through the trees: "Attention, dear, dear students," she began. What? Dooley had done it? Unbelievable! Claudius felt part of his brain mellowing. He had been very cranky and hadn't even realized it.

And look—Mr. Sneed and Elvira were climbing down from the top of the tower.

Metal beams were falling too, and a stray screw landed only a few feet from Claudius's head—although small, it would have likely fractured his skull. But that was nothing compared to the giant metal spike that fell from the sky next.

With no warning, it crashed to the ground like an enormous dart, missing Claudius by inches. The ground quaked from its weight.

Claudius looked up, but it made him dizzy. The tower was so high. Too high.

Wait. Screaming? Did he hear screaming?

Up above. The tower was breaking apart! Wilmer was trapped. Claudius could see him now, clinging to a loose platform, too far to jump to safety. Had Wilmer saved the day only to fall to his doom? Claudius grinned with glee.

He patted his chest, feeling the fabric of the EVIL GENIUS T-shirt hidden under his sweater.

But no. He couldn't let Wilmer die. Maybe it was that radio announcement, which had lightened the weight from Claudius's surly shoulders. Or maybe it was a tinge of regret for cowering here on the ground.

Mr. Sneed and Elvira had reached the bottom of the structure. "I love rainbows," muttered Mr. Sneed.

"I love unicorns," mumbled Elvira.

Claudius eyed the wires sticking out of Mr.

Sneed's back pocket. He couldn't sit here any longer. He could still be a hero. Maybe he could even profit from it. *Claudius!* Now that would be a TV show worth watching.

Claudius gritted his teeth, grabbed the wire from Mr. Sneed's pocket, and bounded toward the radio tower.

"But we can't leave you!" cried Roxie.

"You must!" Wilmer shouted back, clinging to the platform that now hung from a single frayed wire, which was becoming more frayed by the second. "I'm afraid it's frayed," Wilmer moaned. "Remember me fondly."

"I will!" screamed Roxie.

"I'll remember you more!" sobbed Harriet.

Wilmer swallowed a large wad of sorrowful spit, but it was quickly replaced by a gurgle. Someone was scurrying up to the landing from the stairs below. Claudius! What was he doing here? Wasn't he afraid of heights? Or had he found the strength merely to gloat and watch Wilmer plunge to his doom?

"What do *you* want?" yelled Wilmer.

"To save you!" screamed Claudius. He was circling a piece of wire like a rodeo star waves a lariat. Claudius released one end of the wire, and it sailed toward Wilmer. The makeshift lasso stretched out over the empty air and wrapped around the railing just above him.

"Climb across!" screamed Claudius.

Wilmer stared, wide-eyed. Was he dreaming? Maybe it was a trick.

"Hurry!" screamed Claudius.

Wilmer wasn't a particularly experienced wire climber. A scientist needed calm, confident hands, and getting calluses or cuts might hinder the ability to delicately handle test tubes. So, despite strong fingertips, he had always avoided grabbing ropes and monkey bars. He regretted that now. A scientist must be ready for anything, including activities that demanded strong hand climbing. He took a deep breath, grabbed the wire, and inched his way forward.

"Faster!" shouted Roxie.

"I don't have a lot of hand-climbing experience," explained Wilmer. "I'm going as quickly as I can."

One hand after the other. That was the secret. Wilmer ignored the pain from the wire cutting into his palms and fingers. But he was making progress! And if he didn't look down—where he could see that if he slipped, he would land on a slab of rusted, twisted metal that would surely slice him in two— he could almost imagine getting out of this alive.

Wilmer's hands were sweating now. A simple case of a hyperactive sympathetic nervous system, which causes glands in the hands to produce sweat in times of stress or nervousness. It was why Wilmer's hands often felt clammy when he was near Roxie.

Most people's lives flash before their eyes when they are facing death. For Wilmer, information about sweat glands passed before his. He sighed.

Creak. Snap. Wilmer heard it from behind him. He was now dangling directly from the middle of the wire. When you're hovering over nothing but air and a single slip means falling to your death, you don't want to hear creaking or snapping.

Wilmer peeked back. The platform above him split in half. The wire gave way. His stomach lurched. This was it. He flung his hand out in one desperate grab of air, although he knew it was in vain. Good-bye, life.

Hello, hand? Someone snagged Wilmer's flailing palm.

Vlad! His outstretched hand was wrapped around Wilmer's like a momma bear hugging her cub. Vlad pulled Wilmer toward him, up and up. Wilmer's sweaty hands were beginning to slip from Vlad's. Curse that sympathetic nervous system! But Vlad readjusted his grasp and continued to lift Wilmer. Vlad was surprisingly strong. "I've got you."

Wilmer didn't breathe until he was on the platform next to his friends. He hugged the floor. Somehow he had survived. "Thank you! You guys saved my life!" he gushed to Vlad and Claudius.

"Yeah, yeah, yeah. I couldn't let you guys get all the glory," Vlad griped. "What are you looking at?" he yapped at Claudius, who seemed more surprised than anyone.

"Oh, Wilmy! I thought I'd lost you!" gurgled Harriet, buckets of tears pouring down her cheeks. "Hold me!"

"Maybe later?" suggested Wilmer. "Or not. Let's get down from here."

"My hero!" gushed Harriet.

Wilmer dashed down the remaining stairs, which shook and buckled but held together. The others followed behind him.

They hit the ground running. Seconds after they touched earth, the rest of the tower teetered, buckled, and completely collapsed, like a human pyramid after a particularly forceful sneeze from the bottom row.

"We've done it!" yelled Roxie. "Safe at last."

But Wilmer wasn't so sure; he had a horrible thought. If the screeching loudspeakers had cracked the steel tower beams, then the deafening sounds could have done the same to the hotel's foundation. That would explain all the shifting walls and creaking crevices.

And if the radio tower had just collapsed, then the hotel might be next!

"We need to get back!" shouted Wilmer. "I think all the kids at the Sac à Puces are in terrible danger!"

CHAPTER TWENTY-NINE

YOUR SAFETY COMES FIRST!
THE SAC À PUCES PALLADIUM, LODGE, AND
RESORTLIKE HOTEL IS BUILT TO
WITHSTAND FLOODING, EARTHQUAKES,
TORNADOS, WILD ELEPHANTS,
AND LOCUSTS. IF, HOWEVER, SOMETHING
OTHER THAN FLOODING, EARTHQUAKES,
TORNADOS, WILD ELEPHANTS,
AND LOCUSTS COMES ALONG, WE CAN'T
MAKE ANY GUARANTEES.

Wilmer raced through the forest toward the hotel. As he ran, he wasn't thinking about how they had narrowly escaped sure death from a destroyed radio tower. Or how his archenemies had unexpectedly saved him. Or how he had identified the cause of the collapsing radio tower through observation.

No, he was thinking that the reason he was running so fast was because his adrenal glands, which release hormones under stress, were raising his heart rate, blood pressure, and breathing rate, allowing him to run faster than usual.

Yes, Wilmer would make a very good doctor someday.

Behind Wilmer ran Roxie, side-by-side with Harriet. Just thinking of Roxie made Wilmer's adrenal glands shift into an even higher gear.

They soon arrived at the hotel grounds. Part of the roof had collapsed, over where the audio control room had been, but no one seemed to notice. Kids wandered about hugging each other, some walking into the hotel without worry.

"Dr. Dill!" screamed Wilmer when he saw the famous doctor standing on the lawn.

"Why, hello, Wilmer. Claudius. And Vlad!"

"We've defeated Mr. Sneed and Elvira," explained Wilmer. "And Claudius and Vlad saved my life. They're heroes."

Dr. Dill smiled. "Of course they are." He playfully messed up Claudius's hair. "Good job, son."

Claudius grinned wildly.

"But it's not over. You have to help us!" urged

Wilmer. "Tell the kids to get out of the hotel. It's going to collapse!"

Dr. Dill gasped. "A collapsing hotel? Oh my!" He turned and looked at the building, which swayed and shuddered. "Yes, that does look dangerous." Then his phone rang and he answered it with a panicked tone. "Dill here! I can't talk because . . . What? He has Chowder Head? Are his hands clammy?" He rushed off.

Wilmer shook his head in frustration. But he couldn't stand around head-shaking. Not now. Not with so many lives at stake.

Mrs. Valveeta Padgett sat on the ground, writing on a notepad. It was hard to concentrate with so many kids walking around, hugging and shouting happily to each other. They should use their inside voices, even when they were outside. Life would be so much more pleasant that way.

"Mrs. Padgett!" someone yelled. Who was that? Wilmer Dooley? She cringed. What did that boy want now? He was like a rash you couldn't get rid of, no matter how much ointment you slathered on top of it. "You have to help us warn the kids. The hotel is falling. Everyone will be crushed!"

Mrs. Padgett eyed them sternly. She was working on her new script. Shows must have scripts. Did Wilmer think it was easy to write TV shows comparing mah-jongg to whale blubber? If he did, he was wrong. Very wrong.

"Please!" pleaded Roxie. "You have to help us."

Mrs. Padgett arched an eyebrow. "I'm a famous TV star. I don't *have* to do anything." It was then that she noticed Claudius and Vlad for the first time. She blinked and arched her eyebrows even higher. Claudius was working with Wilmer *again*? When would he learn? "I'm very disappointed in you, Claudius."

Claudius lifted his chin up. "If you're disappointed that I'm saving kids from certain death, then that's your problem. You can clean your own wastebaskets next year."

Mrs. Padgett gasped. TV celebrities didn't empty wastebaskets, thank you. The mere idea was horrifying. "Certainly you jest!"

Claudius shook his head. "I never jest."

Which was quite true. Claudius had no sense of humor, really. That was one of the reasons she liked him. "Very well," Mrs. Padgett said after a deep, sorrowful sigh. "I can't get a thing done with all this commotion, anyway."

Besides, maybe she could write a show about mah-jongg and building collapses. Yes, that idea did have some promise.

Wilmer didn't stop to thank his former biology teacher. He needed to get into that hotel and warn the kids. He shoved his way through the front door. It came off its hinges when he pushed it and banged to the ground.

Ernie. He stood across the lobby, holding his nose and wobbling around. He must have just woken up from being clobbered by Harriet earlier. "Ernie! Are you okay?"

"My nose hurts."

"Harriet smacked you pretty hard. You were trying to kill me."

"I was trying to kill you?" Ernie gasped. "Harriet hit me?" He gasped again. "What are you talking about?"

"I'll explain everything later," said Wilmer. "But right now you need to get out of the hotel. The entire place is going to cave in." He turned and yelled, "Everyone get out! Hurry!" But the kids continued hugging and talking and ignoring Wilmer. No one rushed to escape, despite the crumbling walls around them. "Get out! Now!" Wilmer yelled again, but no one paid him any attention.

Then an electronic squawk rang through the air. Wilmer's eardrums tingled. Had Elvira and Mr. Sneed recovered? Were they about to transmit some horrible order to the kids? Where were his earplugs, anyway?

"Listen up, students," said a crackling voice that boomed through the room. "The hotel is about to collapse. Flee! Hurry!"

Kids heard *that*. They rushed toward the exits, hurtling themselves out of the building. As they did, part of the roof caved in. A large chunk of concrete smashed onto the floor. A dresser from the room above dropped with it, right through a coffee table.

Wilmer and his friends turned and ran, joining the throngs of kids escaping the building.

"Get out! Faster!" urged Mrs. Padgett. She stood on the lawn and shouted into a bullhorn. Her warnings rang out through the grounds.

Behind Wilmer, Lizzy and Tizzy—the very last people in the building, it turned out—flung themselves out the open door just as the entire hotel fell in upon itself and flattened like a concrete pancake.

"My goodness!" exclaimed Mrs. Padgett. "Good thing I found this old bullhorn lying around— imagine what might have happened."

Wilmer exhaled deeply. But there was still one piece of unfinished business.

Roxie stood next to him. He cleared his throat and took a step toward her. This would be the bravest thing he had ever done. Braver than scaling a tower. Braver than standing up to Mr. Sneed. Braver than running into a collapsing hotel. "Roxie?" he blurted out.

"Yes?" she asked, looking up, her eyes twinkling from the sun shining above.

Harriet stepped directly into his line of sight. She stood fifteen micrometers away, possibly less.

She took Wilmer's hand in hers and held it gently. "We need to talk, Wilmy."

"Um, maybe later?" muttered Wilmer.

Harriet tightened her grip on his hand. "I'm afraid this can't wait." Why was she puckering her lips? Was it because she was deep in thought, or maybe—?

Please let it be because she was deep in thought. Wilmer looked down at her nervously. "Look, about us—"

"Hush," Harriet interrupted, putting a finger over Wilmer's mouth with one hand while gently rubbing his palm with the other. "I need to tell you something. I still think you're an amazing scientist. But I realize now that physics and sound waves are my true calling. Food biology just doesn't excite me like it does you. I'm sorry. I think we should go our separate ways. We're not meant for each other."

"Really?" said Wilmer. "Uh, okay." He grinned. "Besides, I want to be a doctor."

Harriet threw her arms around Wilmer, squeezing so hard that the air was knocked out of his lungs. "Thank you for taking it so well. I know it must be hard on you. You'll always have a special place in my heart." She released her embrace and Wilmer took a big gulp of air.

Harriet walked away. Roxie looked up from the pad of paper she held, where she had furiously been taking notes. "This will make the best *Mumpley Musings* radio report ever," she gushed. She looked at Wilmer. "Maybe you can guest host?"

"Really? Me?" Wilmer's adrenal glands pumped with glee. Roxie never had guest hosts on her show. Wilmer could barely imagine such bliss. "I mean, if you really want me."

"Are you kidding? The Amazing Wilmer Dooley?" she said with a wink.

"Can you not call me that?" asked Wilmer. "I want to be just regular old Wilmer Dooley if it's okay with you."

Roxie smiled broadly. "I like that even better. Maybe you can come over to my house this week and we can write the show together?"

Wilmer practically fainted as he nodded his head up and down, up and down, so quickly and furiously that he stopped when he feared his head might roll off his neck.

His dreams of eternal happiness were awoken when Dr. Dill strode up to them. "He has Rib Eye?" he screamed into his phone. "My, those are rare...." He kept walking without even a wave.

"I'll be starting school with you in a couple of weeks," snapped Vlad, eyeing Wilmer with a very unfriendly sneer. Wilmer had been so lost in heavenly Roxie-land that he had forgotten about Vlad and Claudius. "I saved your life, but this doesn't mean we're friends."

"Of course not," agreed Wilmer.

"That goes double for me," scowled Claudius.

"That goes triple for me," piped in Ernie, stepping forward. Then he wheeled around and shot out his thumb. Wilmer quickly gave him a vigorous best-friend thumbshake.

"I hope you're not mad at me, Ernie," Wilmer said. "I promised we'd hang out all weekend, and I'm afraid I wasn't a very good friend. I let my head get too big."

"Well, I'm sorry for trying to kill you," said Ernie. "I suppose that makes us even."

Mrs. Padgett cleared her throat. She stared at the destroyed hotel. "A shame," she muttered to herself. "Such a lovely hotel. Well, not lovely. Not even nice. But it was a hotel."

"Who won the science fair?" asked Roxie.

Mrs. Padgett looked startled. "I completely forgot. I was hired to judge a contest, and I suppose I should do my job. Let no one accuse Valveeta Padgett of dropping the ball!" She wandered toward the rubble, stepping over shards of twisted metal and concrete boulders.

Something shone in the middle of the debris— a faint electric light. Mrs. Padgett made her way toward the glow and cleared some fallen drywall from around it. She lifted up a small object. Wires led from a light bulb into a potato.

"Hey, it worked," said Ernie, as surprised as anyone.

"I hereby give Ernie Rinehart first place in this year's state science fair!" declared Mrs. Padgett.

She walked out of the rubble, took a mangled ribbon from her pocket, and handed it to Ernie.

"Wow, thanks!" he exclaimed.

"I guess that makes you the greatest middle-school scientist in the state," said Wilmer.

"That's me," agreed Ernie with a laugh. "I'm a regular Alfred Einstern."

"That's *Albert* Ein*stein*," said Wilmer.

Ernie shrugged. "Him too."

CHAPTER THIRTY

**THE FORTY-FIFTH ANNUAL STATE
SCIENCE FAIR AND CONSORTIUM!**
The First Place Medal
for Scientific Achievement goes to

Ernie Rinehart
for his entry

"Electric Potato"
Official Judge

Valveeta Padgett

Wilmer waved good-bye to Roxie and Harriet as they climbed into Roxie's dad's car. "I think our radio show will be a smash hit," said Roxie. "And don't forget to call me. I waited all summer and you never did."

Wilmer nodded, although part of him—the incredibly wimpy part—was already trying to think of an excuse not to get in touch with her. What if the radio show went poorly? What if the script was bad? What if he broke the microphone? Or sneezed on her? Roxie might never speak to him again. Maybe it was best to avoid calling her and to continue playing hard to get.

Not that he *was* hard to get. He was pretty easy to get when it came to Roxie.

No. He *would* call her. Avoiding Roxie—that was the old Wilmer. But calling her wasn't the newer, bad Wilmer either. It was a brand-new Wilmer that was mostly the old Wilmer but with a new, more confident part. Maybe.

Wilmer shook his head. It didn't feel cloudy anymore, but he was terribly confused, anyway.

"It's been great getting to know you," said Harriet, wiping a lone tear from her cheek. "I still think you're amazing, even if we aren't meant for each other."

Parents were picking up their kids, shocked to find a destroyed hotel and to hear about the horrible plot. With no landlines or cell phone service (except for Dr. Dill's special phone, and he hadn't been any help at all), there had been no way to contact the outside world. Parents were angry to hear about what had happened, but it was hard to stay mad at Mr. Sneed and Elvira when they were so busy wishing everyone to "Have a wonderful rainbow day!" and exclaiming, "We love unicorns!"

Mr. Dooley hurried over from the parking lot with a loud shout and a hearty wave. He wore one shoe, his pants backward, and oversize goggles that extended about six inches from his face. "Wilmer! Ernie! There you are! How was your weekend? Did you indulge in the splendor of science?"

"Um, Dad, the hotel is destroyed," said Wilmer, pointing to the debris.

"Oh? Why, so it is. I didn't notice. I hope that didn't spoil things for you. Are you ready to go? Mom is cooking up a wonderful dinner tonight just for you. Something with furniture wax and tartar sauce. She's been very secretive about it. But Preston has been proudly shouting 'red pepper flakes' all morning, so I think it's spicy. That's called observation. All scientists have the talent."

Wilmer nodded. His dad hadn't noticed the fallen hotel, of course, but Wilmer was used to his selective observations.

"It was a very interesting weekend," said

Ernie as they walked to the car. "I won first place at the fair." He held up his ribbon.

"Congratulations!" shouted Mr. Dooley, giving Ernie a slap on the back. "I always knew you had it in you."

They passed Dr. Dill, who was off his phone and standing with Vlad and Claudius. The cousins scowled when the Dooleys and Ernie approached.

"Why, hello, Fernando!" Mr. Dooley greeted Dr. Dill. "I heard that you were chaperoning this weekend. I trust the kids didn't give you any trouble?"

"Of course not. I watched them like a hawk. Vlad is a marvelous child."

"And so is Claudius, right?" asked Mr. Dooley, patting Claudius on the head.

"Of course," said Dr. Dill. "That goes without saying." Claudius smiled just as his father's phone rang. Dr. Dill answered it. "Dr. Dill here . . . What? She has the Belly Flops? Are you sure you're not jumping to conclusions?" Without another glance, he walked away in animated conversation.

Wilmer, Ernie, and Dr. Dooley strolled through the parking lot. "I think it's wonderful that Dr. Dill spent the weekend with Claudius," said Mr. Dooley. "I hope you aren't mad that I couldn't come too."

"Of course not. I wouldn't trade you for Dr. Dill or any other father in the world," said Wilmer.

Mr. Dooley blushed. Wilmer almost made a comment about how blushing is caused by adrenaline and blood flow, but then decided that no one probably cared.

"I hope you got my note," said Mr. Dooley. "I hid a special one for you in your shoe."

"I did, Dad. And it was helpful. The power of observation goes a long way. It was just the reminder that I needed."

"I'm glad to hear it," said Mr. Dooley. "I would have felt terrible if anything went wrong this weekend."

They strolled past a chain of ambulances parked in front of the hotel, their sirens blaring. Three fire trucks were behind them, and dozens of firefighters ran around shouting and sifting through the rubble.

"Yes, it's a good thing nothing went wrong," said Wilmer with a sigh.

As Ernie and Wilmer climbed into the back of Mr. Dooley's car, Wilmer saw something wedged between the seats. He lifted out a small yellow candy wrapped in clear plastic. A handwritten note read, *May your weekend be filled with happiness and sardines.* "This must have fallen out of my pocket during the drive up," said Wilmer.

Ernie snatched the bar from Wilmer's hands without looking at the note, ripped open the package, and snapped off a giant bite. Within seconds, he was rolling down the window and spitting out the treat, his face looking as yellow as the candy.

"Mom's chocolate-sardine-lemon wraps," said Wilmer with a sympathetic nod.

Ernie gasped for air as Mr. Dooley pulled the car out of the parking space. Wilmer looked outside the window and saw Mr. Sneed shouting to one of the firefighters. "Of course! Who doesn't love unicorns?"

Dear Journal,

It was a long weekend. I'm looking forward to some peace and quiet at home. All scientists need their rest. Einstein supposedly slept ten hours a night unless he was in the middle of a great discovery. And then he slept eleven hours a night.

I'm grateful for the power of observation. Once again, it saved the day. But there is something even more important than observation, not only in science, but everywhere. Friendship. I wouldn't have saved anyone without help from Harriet, Roxie, Ernie, and even Claudius and Vlad. If anyone calls me "amazing" for saving the hotel, I'll make sure I give all of them proper credit. They're ALL amazing.

I'm through with being the hero, anyway. I just want to be a normal seventh grader this year.

Uh-oh. The car just stalled. Dad says it must be from the new purple GasBUZZZZ! he poured into the fuel tank after he arrived. Not all of Dad's ideas are great. A few months ago he invented Barf-BUZZZZ! It was worse than it sounds.

Uh-oh again . . . Dad says we need to get out of

the car right now before it blows up. Not a good sign.
I'll write more later. When I begin my normal life.
Which will be soon, I hope.

But honestly, probably never.

Signing off,

Me

ACKNOWLEDGMENTS

First and foremost, I would like to acknowledge myself, without whom this book would not exist. Really, anyone else I'm acknowledging is far down the list of responsible parties.

Still, I must mention Emma Ledbetter, editor extraordinaire, who is single-handedly responsible for elevating this book to its almost embarrassingly lofty heights, as well as Joanna Volpe: agent, cheerleader, and world record holder in Bozo Buckets.

I would also like to express my eternal thanks to Lauren, Emmy, Madelyn, and various relatives, in-laws, and such. You are all dear to me, unless you aren't. I'll be in touch.

And no acknowledgment of mine can fail to mention the marvelous mustache of Chester A. Arthur, our twenty-first president. To those who say William Howard Taft had a more impressive display of facial hair, I denounce you! Shame!

—F. D.